BUBBLEGUM CHRONICLES
Runaway Evolution

GABRIEL MCDONALD

Printed in the United States of America
Library of Congress Control Number: 2025921545
ISBN: Softcover 978-1-969213-26-7
e-Book 978-1-969213-27-4
Published by: TwinVerse Prime
Publication Date: 10/01/2025

To order copies of this book, contact:
TwinVerse Prime
Phone: (725) 257-6538
clients@twinverseprime.com
www.twinverseprime.com/

TABLE OF CONTENTS

*"Take no part in the unfruitful works of darkness,
but instead expose them." - Ephesians 5:11*

DEDICATION

For my beloved sons, Gabriel and Jericho McDonald, far away in Scottsdale, Arizona: In the midst of chaos and shadows, you are the beacon that guides my soul. Like the heroes who fight for peace in these pages, may you always carry bravery in your hearts and find strength in love when the world feels uncertain.

This story is a promise: No matter what storms come, hope endures, and so do you.

CHAPTER ONE

HEADQUARTERS

Sacramento, California. March 10th.

It's been nearly five months since our last encounter with Winston Boswell and the Revival. I know I should be at peace with our accomplishments as we rebuild our country. The families that were once in hiding have been given a second chance, and together they have broken free from the shackles that burdened them for so long.

The Chronicles has become much more than just a team of misfit mutants. We are now respected among the people we have saved, and our name has become a beacon of hope for the innocent. Even with the evil that lurks through the darkness, the enemy now knows there will be consequences for their actions.

During our extensive journey I have come to accept who I am and who I have become. Each morning, I relive my moments on Mystic Cloud as I gaze into the sky of blue. Feeling God's presence has given me the strength and the courage I needed to become the leader I was meant to be.

E.C.H.O. has assisted us in clearing out the memory of Boswell's war. James Hawthorne and I have also become very close over the last several months, and our relationship is now common knowledge. Although things between us are strictly professional. Maintaining discipline is a factor that we can't ignore.

As I write this, I can't help but think of all the battles we've been through and the many more we've stopped from happening. My final memory of Dr. Eugene Maximus has been keeping me up at night. I can't begin to forgive myself for his passing. The memory of him will forever be a wound that reopens at the mention of his name. I will always consider him to be my real father, and I thank him for gifting us Machine.

There's still much that needs to be done. The enemy never sleeps, and we need to remain alert so that we always come out victorious. Take one day at a time here. Never forget your roots. And always pray for a peaceful outcome. I leave this passage until another time and hope that our people will remain safe. With God, all things are possible. - Crescendo.

Jasmine sat at her desk glaring at her diary. She felt overwhelmed at times with her thoughts but still confident of what the future had in store for them. She pulled her attention away from the desk to a mirror across the room. She stared at her reflection, feeling full of knowledge but tired from the endless battles. Jasmine always felt a sudden boost when she was surrounded by the ones she grew to love and those that had fought beside her during the war.

Jasmine turned away from the mirror, standing up and placing her hair into a ponytail. She approached the window and looked out across the parking lot that had been built into a fortress. A slight grin came over her as she leaned out the window watching the civilians work and patrol the area. Hawthorne was standing with Captain Pike examining a watchtower they had just built.

The shouting of hard-working men and women from across the property gave her reassurance that everyone was growing stronger together. Lawman the engineer was hanging from the side of the tower, strapped up and welding, while Hawthorne shouted to him from below, "That's good for now! Come on down!"

Lawman shouted back, "I'm not finished yet!"

Hawthorne wasn't arguing with the help. "If you weren't so damn slow, the job could've been finished today! Now get down here!"

Pike grinned while directing Hawthorne away from the tower. "Just leave him be."

Hawthorne stepped away with him. "Why are you siding with that joker?"

Pike stated the facts: "Lawman created the Gun House on the Kingdom. That's what was used to slaughter the Scrapers at Homeland that day. Trust me, he knows what he's doing."

Hawthorne gave him a stern stare. "I'd rather not talk about that. Those were the days you and Lawman were against us."

Pike hated the memory of it: "Water under a bridge."

Hawthorne stopped and watched Lawman come down the tower with his equipment. "This place is looking pretty good. I would be lying if I said we didn't owe it to you and your friends. I misjudged you, Pike. I hope you accept that as an apology for giving you a hard time because that's the best you're going to get."

Pike smirked, "I wasn't expecting anything at all."

Lawman wiped the sweat from his brow and left the equipment behind. He jogged over, catching up with them. "Every day it's the same thing. How much more are we going to build onto this place? Boswell hasn't shown himself in months. It's over."

Hawthorne corrected him, "It's never over. Crescendo knows that, too. We're waiting for Boswell's replacement. There's always someone to fight."

Lawman snapped his fingers when he remembered, "This is about Prestige, right?"

Pike reached out to pat Lawman across the back. "Try not to say that name too loudly. It'll put people on edge."

"But she got away. That means she's still out there." Lawman couldn't shake it from his mind.

Pike nodded. "That's true, but from what I heard, Prestige had her hands full after meeting Crescendo. I doubt she'll come around looking for trouble. Crescendo will need to find her."

Hawthorne pointed to Lawman. "He's right, and by the way, you're on the watch tonight. You've been skipping day shifts for a week. Don't think I don't know what's going on here."

Lawman asked, "Will I be in the new watchtower?"

Pike volunteered, "I'll take the first night with him. He could use the extra pair of eyes."

Hawthorne didn't see any harm in it. "Fine. Just don't make it a habit." Hawthorne saw Jasmine hanging outside the window upstairs. "Something on your mind, Crescendo?"

She squinted her eyes at him. "I love it when you're moody. You should call it a day. There's always tomorrow."

Pike turned around and scanned the property at the patrolling guards. "Get some rest. We can handle this."

Hawthorne made note of his suspicious behavior: "Why are you in such a good mood?"

"I figured one of us should be," he cunningly replied. Pike couldn't help but wonder about the enemy. "Now that he mentioned it, there's no telling what the Revival is doing. Maybe they're waiting for the Chronicles to try going for them again."

Jasmine watched them from the window above. "Anything's possible. Just don't let your guard down. The last thing we need is another repeat of Boswell."

Hawthorne sarcastically added, "I was having a peaceful day before you brought this up." He turned to push Lawman away. "Good job!"

Pike wouldn't let it go. "It's been too long. Why isn't Boswell making a move?"

Hawthorne suggested, "Maybe Prestige won't allow him. From what I've been hearing, she's calling the shots in that family."

Moments later Redford drove her Deathtrap into the parking lot, taking up two spaces. She brought the vehicle to a halting stop and shut off the engine. Pike stared at the bed of the truck at their latest addition to the team. A parting gift from the late Dr. Maximus. Pike pointed to Machine while still trying to get used to his size and appearance. "Was he useful for you out there today?"

Redford dropped out of the vehicle, taking her sunglasses off. "You writing a book?"

He wasn't surprised with the remark. Redford was just that moody person everyone loved to have around in case things got serious. She knew how to handle herself. As she approached him, they shook hands. Pike grinned. "You always were a smartass."

She brushed her fire-red hair behind her shoulders while giving orders to Machine: "Get the tools and bring them inside for me."

The machine dropped out onto his feet. The Deathtrap sprang up after the weight of the machine stepped off. He stood at seven feet tall and was upgraded with enhanced weapons and vision. Machine reached in the back of the truck and pulled out a couple of duffle bags full of tools. He greeted Pike while passing by, "Good evening, Pike. I trust you've had a good day."

He stepped aside, giving Machine room to pass. "It's always a pleasure to see you."

Machine walks further away from them, saying, "Thank you, same to you."

Redford took notice of the recent changes. "I see Lawman finally finished the tower."

Pike nodded. "Yeah, do you like it?"

She smirked, "It could be better."

Lawman shrugged his shoulders. "I'm standing right here."

Redford sarcastically replied, "Yes, you are."

Hawthorne was satisfied that progress was at least being made: "It's an improvement."

Redford knew Hawthorne was sensitive about the time he and Jasmine were spending together. So, she made sure to make a comment: "Any idea where Crescendo is, Hawthorne? I was hoping to speak with her later. I've noticed you two have been going over plans and making your daily rounds together."

Pike smirked, "She said it, not me."

Lawman backed away from the group. "I'll go find something to do."

Hawthorne stood with a scowl on his face. "You do that."

Redford changed the subject, filling them in on her trip. "Wrench asked if I could find him some extra tools. So, Machine and I went out to get some from our friend downtown. It's nice to finally be able to leave the base without getting shot at for a change."

Pike agreed, "If Boswell were here, he wouldn't believe that his soldiers surrendered and are now working for us."

Redford laughed. "Everyone left Boswell the first chance they got! I don't blame them!"

Pike reminded them, "I was one of them. The man's insane. I think it was risky allowing them to work alongside us, but Hawthorne felt differently."

Hawthorne stood firm. "My men haven't had any problems. They're well supervised and trained. Besides, they seem to have changed after being set free from the burdens of Boswell's war. They deserve a second chance. Working with E.C.H.O. is their privilege."

Redford gawked at him. "You're spending far too much time with Crescendo. You're getting soft, Hawthorne."

He swallowed his original response and kept it clean: "Boswell's men are now our men. We began with about a dozen soldiers and now have nearly three hundred over a course of six months. That's an accomplishment to be proud of."

Machine returned to the group asking, "Who's Boswell?"

Pike answered, "He's an evil man and hopefully just a bad memory from here on."

Machine: "That's good. Bad men bring death."

"You're absolutely right." He turned to Redford. "You can find Wrench in the back shop making a racket as usual."

Redford passed through them. "Thanks. Come on, Machine. Let's go bother senile."

Hawthorne reached out to pat Pike across the shoulder before walking away. "Keep your eyes peeled. I'll be upstairs if you need me."

Pike stepped further out into the parking lot and instantly caught the scent of a fragrance he would never forget. He heard a woman's voice calling out to him, "Did you miss me, Captain?"

Pike turned and saw Victoria Hendrix sitting on the hood of one of the vehicles. She sat with her legs crossed, casually chewing her bubblegum without a care in the world. He shook his head, baffled by her demeanor. "You're always showing up when I least expect it."

She raised her eyebrows while sliding off the hood of the car. "That's the best time." Hendrix reached over to straighten his uniform for him. "So, where's my big strong man heading off to?"

"Nowhere, I'm keeping an eye on things out here. I could use the fresh air. It's hectic inside. Somehow Crescendo's managed to invite every person she meets to our base."

"That's who she is. She saves people. I thought you'd catch on by now."

Pike seemed exhausted. "I know, but we need to keep an eye on everyone. We're outnumbered. Hawthorne's allowed Boswell's men to work for us, too. Things are getting crazy around here."

Hendrix agreed, "Crescendo's getting closer to Hawthorne. They're the leaders. Follow them or make your own team. There's no other choice."

Pike set the record straight: "I'll never go against them. I just want things to cool down for a bit. I can feel something about to happen."

Hendrix interrupted, "Boswell is on all our minds, not just yours. Every day until we take our last breath, we will expect him to reappear again unless he's dead. That's the way it is. Live with it or kill him."

Pike smirked, "You're in a good mood today."

She smiled. "I've also had a lot on my mind. That's why I went away for a couple of days. Nowhere special. I just needed time to think. It's nice that we can safely travel alone again. Remember that for the next time you want to come down on Crescendo and Hawthorne's leadership. They made it possible for us to roam freely without fear." Hendrix rubbed Pike's chest, staring deep into his eyes. "It's good to see you again." They stood like that for a moment. After breaking the connection, Hendrix walked away, leaving him standing there with his imagination.

On the inside of the factory, Jasmine remained in her room. After hearing a knock at her door, she sprang up and answered it. "I was wondering what took you so long, James." She pulled Hawthorne inside and shut the door.

He took off his utility belt and placed it on the end of her bed before sitting down. "Today ends our final improvements. It's about time too."

Jasmine sat alongside him. "You're overworking yourself. We have enough men. Have someone take over for you."

"Pike takes care of that for me. He's getting to be one of our own."

Jasmine reached over, grabbing hold of his hand. "How do Bergman and the others feel about him? I know it took a while for them to say more than a few words to him."

Hawthorne was thrilled to say they were over it. "They know he's still learning. Pike tries hard enough to be helpful but maintains a distance to not lose his own way. We respect that. As long as we're on the same page, that's all that matters." He swiftly added, "Besides, Hendrix is taking a liking to Pike. I'd rather not get involved."

Jasmine chuckled, "Hendrix will scratch your eyes out for Pike!"

Hawthorne stood up and paced the room. "What are we doing here, Crescendo?"

"What do you mean?" A look of concern came over her.

"You seemed so sure of yourself back when it was just Boswell we were facing. And now there's this other person."

"What are you trying to say?"

He stopped dead in his tracks, explaining, "Now there's two of them. When will this end? It's never really over until they've been brought to justice. Isn't that what you say to us?"

"I can only do what I can. The rest is in God's hands."

Hawthorne answered right back, "Maybe that's the problem. We need to let God handle it all and do nothing."

Jasmine rose to her feet and stared out the window. "Are you suggesting God will bring us the answer if we just carry on business as usual? That doesn't sound like you, James."

He grinned. "I've been accused of turning into you. We spend so much time together these days."

Jasmine already knew who it was. "Is Cinder giving you a hard time?"

"If she didn't, I would think something was wrong."

She turned around, taking a long look at Hawthorne. "I'm grateful for this time together. Who knows when something will happen?"

"I just hope we're all prepared for it when it does come." Hawthorne shook the thought from his mind. "How does the Revival family make the mark it did?"

Jasmine replied, "It's simple. There wasn't anyone willing enough to stop them."

Hawthorne stated, "Until the Chronicles."

Jasmine reached out, grabbing him and pulling him forward. She raised herself onto her tiptoes to kiss him gently on the lips. "We couldn't have done this without you."

He kissed her back while sarcastically replying, "Don't forget it." They hugged each other and remained still and quiet for a moment. Hawthorne broke the silence. "You're the one keeping this together. The people believe in you, Crescendo. You gave them hope. I remember how different it was back at Homeland. We've all come a long way."

She lowered her head. "It's nice to be needed." She smirked. "We've been here before, James, speaking about the past and unsure of what the future will bring. Whatever happens, promise me we'll keep each other strong."

He let her go and kissed her forehead. He locked eyes with her, shaking his head. "I'm not going anywhere." He proposed an idea: "In fact, the rest of the team is still at the military base for the night. They'll be covered for now."

She knew where he was heading. "What are you saying?"

"I can stay with you tonight if you like."

Jasmine placed her hands on her hips with an offended stare in her eyes. "James Hawthorne, I should slap you for even suggesting this!"

He took a step back with his arms up. "I only thought you could use the company. You seem as exhausted as I feel."

She walked towards him, leading to the door. "I knew exactly what you thought." He opened it and stepped out as she stood at the threshold shaking her head in disbelief. "If I ever get that kind of company from you, there better be wedding bells ringing in the distance first." She raised her eyebrows at him before shutting the door. "Good evening, James." After hearing the sound of footsteps walking away, Jasmine leaned against the door, smiling at the thought of it.

CHAPTER TWO

THE REVIVAL

El Paso, Texas.

The second property owned by the family was heavily guarded. Extra precautions had been taken since their last encounter with the Chronicles. Prestige sat outside, calming her nerves with some champagne. Her mind was racing with the endless possibilities for family if they could accomplish their goals in the near future. They were well within the reach of true greatness.

Prestige heard someone coming up from behind, "Come join me, Brawler. It's a beautiful evening." She smiled at the thought of her bright future.

Brawler approached a chair opposite of a table with her champagne and charcuterie board. He sat down as she ate some cheese. "I'm surprised to see you in such a good mood. A few days ago, you were killing some of our own men after arguing with them about the Chronicles."

Prestige crossed her legs while chewing her cheese. "Today I'm focused on other things. Besides, the Revival has faced many trials and tribulations over the years. Each time we've come out victorious. You worry too much."

Brawler watched her sit there elegantly dressed in her power blue dress with a fierce stare in her eyes. "Pardon me for asking, but do you know what you're doing?"

She pointed to the board. "Have you tried this cheese? It's good."

"You don't seem to be bothered by any of this. I guess I shouldn't be talking about it unless you mention it first." He politely added, "My apologies."

She suddenly asked, "Are you concerned for me?"

"I'm here to make sure you're safe, remember."

She assured him, "I know what I'm doing."

He didn't argue with her, "You always do."

She heard a sign of worry in his voice, "You don't agree with my plans, do you?"

He didn't want her to think he was getting cold feet. "I never said that."

"I know, but it seems like all my help is starting to feel as if we're wasting our time here." Prestige shook her head repeatedly. "That would be a shame. The Revival family has never backed down before, and I would be very disappointed to see it happen this time around."

Brawler reached over to grab some champagne for himself. "I don't feel that way at all. I just think that last move we made was a foolish one. We knew the risks with the Chronicles, and yet we allowed them straight in."

Prestige finished her drink and held out her glass so he could pour her some more. "I've always admired your honesty, Brawler. I thank you for that."

"I don't have much else."

She corrected him, "Sure you do. You have me."

"And that's all I need."

Prestige opened up to him, "I've been thinking a lot lately."

"I knew something was on your mind."

She fessed up, "It is true, I did underestimate the Chronicles. That girl is a true leader."

"Her luck will run out," Brawler stated.

"No, not hers. I saw her eyes. I've never seen eyes like that before. Not here anyway." Prestige paused a moment before adding, "Only on Mystic Cloud did I ever see eyes like that. Crescendo is a warrior."

Brawler replied, "You seem to admire them. They destroyed your home in New York."

She corrected him, "No, I destroyed my home in New York. It was time to leave anyway. We have work to do here. I would be lying if I said I wasn't fully concerned, but that's what our soldiers are hired for. No matter what happens, we must stay on track."

Brawler wanted to end it: "If you're concerned, just have them killed. Next time they show up will be different. Poison and I didn't kill them last time because of you."

She was pleased with his loyalty. "If I had an army of men like you, I feel our goals could be achieved even sooner." She took a moment to consider the idea. "Is it possible to end them?"

"We have an army. Just say the word and I'll gather our men and hunt them down." Brawler took a sip of his champagne.

"Hold off any attacks for now. Let's see where this takes us first."

She wasn't through yet.

"Why wait until it's too late? Let me kill them now."

She wasn't ready. "Now isn't the time to attack."

"It's been six months." Brawler was ready to end them.

Prestige finished her drink quickly and set her glass on the table. "I realize that."

Brawler tried thinking of something clever enough to get her attention. "How about that worm Winston Boswell?"

She laughed, "What about him?!"

"It's about time he did something useful. This whole damn thing is his fault anyway. If it weren't for him leaving the Revival family to start a war, we'd never know about the Chronicles. I say we go hunt them down. Boswell can tag along with us to see this through."

"You make a good point, but I still don't think it's wise to make a move just yet."

Brawler sighed, "I don't feel right about this. I don't understand why you refuse to kill them when you can easily do it." He was getting frustrated.

Prestige knew she could never make him fully understand, "You haven't been to Mystic Cloud. You have no idea what it's like. I can't explain it. You don't just kill someone from Mystic Cloud. It's not the same as killing others. These are God's people."

"That's where the portal comes in? You were talking about that before."

Prestige tells him more, "The portal only opens if God allows it. That's why we've come here. It was our time to leave New York. Our destiny begins here."

Brawler arrogantly replied, "Crescendo's not as tough as she thinks. Her friends weren't too impressive either."

Prestige spoke from her own experiences, "Crescendo is a mutant like us. I fought with her. She's pushed by God. I can feel His presence when she's around. I had a taste of a much better life, and now I've been cast down along with my late sister."

Brawler felt sorry for her loss. "It was a tragedy."

Prestige didn't want to think about it. "I was barely able to escape before the place was blown to hell. I was lucky to escape Crescendo."

Brawler was shocked to hear her say that, "No, she was the lucky one."

"It feels like I've known her in another life."

"I doubt it. It's just a feeling," Brawler dismissed it.

Prestige thought about the Chronicles. "By now Crescendo probably changed California. Boswell still had men there he left behind."

"They were probably killed." Brawler had no remorse for blowing up the refueling station.

She disagreed, "No, that's not like Crescendo. They're probably held hostage. Crescendo isn't a killer like us. She couldn't do it."

"There can't be many held hostage. It's not worth the trouble rescuing them. Let them rot."

Prestige grinned. "I've forgotten how cold you can get." She needed something to work with. "Who stands with the Chronicles?"

"Captain Pike is still with them. I know of Victoria Hendrix, Stamina, and Cross. I'm sure there are others, too."

"That's a handful." She wasn't satisfied. "That's not enough."

Brawler went down the list. "There's also Cinder and Remedy, and that Fedora character. We'll have trouble out of him. He has a weapon from hell."

Prestige asked him with all seriousness, "Do you feel confident you could handle them?"

"Of course, they won't be a problem for me."

She needed to be convinced, but at least she was on the fence: "We'll talk about this again."

"I'm here at your disposal whenever you need me. That's why I'm here. Poison feels the same. We have enough help around to obtain our goals."

Prestige changed the subject. "How's the progress coming along with our men?"

Brawler was pleased to inform her, "They've dug as deep as they can go. I don't fully understand the reason behind this gold dust, but this is your show."

"Tell them to dig deeper and spread out as wide as they can go. You don't need to understand what I'm doing just yet. The time will come. Believe it."

He nodded. "Yes, but our men are working around the clock."

"If they're tired, have them replaced by others guarding the compound. We must have more of this material. Keep digging. Don't let them stop. Do you understand me?"

"Yes, I understand." He bowed his head to her.

Prestige was delighted. "It won't be long now."

Brawler finishes his drink and puts the glass down. "The facility might not hold it all if we bring back more material."

"Yes, it will!" She shouted.

"Should I have them replaced, too?"

She didn't care. "It's their job to keep up. If they're falling behind, have them replaced. Do whatever you have to. Just keep them working."

"I don't understand." Brawler gave up on the rest of it. He knew what she wanted; she made it crystal clear.

Prestige filled him in on the secret of the material: "On Mystic Cloud we would speak about this gold dust often. This material is very special. It's taken me a long time to figure out how to return to Mystic Cloud. I've finally figured it out."

"What are you talking about?"

Prestige shut her eyes and tried to remember the last time she spoke of it. "My sister and I would dream about seeing the gold dust. It was better known as Gypsy Dust."

Brawler stands and points out into the field ahead of them, "How did you know where to look for the Gypsy Dust? The material is everywhere. You just need to know what to look for."

"We've had people searching for us already. You've been gone far too long, Brawler. You were with Boswell in California during all this." She needed to include him in the future plans.

Brawler curiously asked, "What is it exactly?"

"The Gypsy Dust came from the hands of God from when He created the heavens and the earth. As He built this world, the Gypsy Dust would fall from His hands like glitter. They would fall across the land and bless His creations as He brought life into this world. The Gypsy Dust has been around since the beginning of time. Only those from Mystic Cloud know about it."

Brawler was starting to understand, "Your entire purpose was to return to Mystic Cloud with your sister to take revenge on God for casting the two of you out? How's my aim?"

She answered, "Impressive, but there's more to it than that. The portals only open by God. Nobody knows when, where, or how long He will have them open. If I gather enough of the Gypsy Dust and use His own power against Him, I'll be able to return to Mystic Cloud."

Brawler respected her but wasn't prepared for this plan. "I'm afraid you'll need to count me out on that. I'll fight Boswell, and I'll even fight the Chronicles, but I draw the line at God."

Prestige was shocked. "You don't think it's possible?" Prestige knew he wasn't willing to believe, "It's only a matter of time before Mystic Cloud will be mine." She thought further into it, "You said you would stand with me regardless of what happens. I can understand why this time you might want to go your separate way."

Brawler paced back and forth for a moment. "And if it goes wrong?"

"It won't." She turned to rub his forearms down. "It won't fail." She stepped behind him to massage his shoulders. "With our men hard at work, it won't be long before I have everything I need. You and Poison will keep everything running smoothly until that time comes. I know it seems like a long shot. Don't lose faith in me, Brawler."

"I'll always have faith in you. Some days are just harder than others," he honestly replied.

She would never forget what happened to her and her sister, the Tempest: "I was cast out from a world of light and brought to this darkness. I'll do anything to get back."

"If Crescendo knew about your plans, she would be here. To be on the safe side, they should be killed before they randomly show up like cockroaches. They can't hurt you if they're dead."

Prestige sighed, "You just keep going until you get your way. You remind me of myself sometimes. Perhaps you need some rest, Brawler. I've overworked you. That's my fault. Take some time off and observe the men from a distance. Keep them working. Don't give me a problem about this. You need to understand what this means to me."

Brawler asked, "If you get to Mystic Cloud, what will happen to the Revival family?"

"I haven't given that any thought." She stopped rubbing his shoulders and sat back down. "Perhaps that's something we should all sit down and talk about."

He shook his head in awe. "That leaves us to face the Chronicles."

"And you can have them killed any way you like." She grinned.

Brawler sat back down and poured some more champagne for her. "I'd rather serve you."

Prestige regretfully replied, "I'm afraid you wouldn't be able to make it to Mystic Cloud. This is a journey I've wanted to go on alone. My sister was supposed to join me, but now she's dead."

Brawler pointed to her. "I'm not taking orders from Boswell again. If you leave, he doesn't run the Revival family. Let's agree on that."

She reached out to shake his hand. "Agreed."

He was sincere with his words: "I'll do whatever I can to keep the family alive."

Prestige reached over to rub his chest. She was feeling the champagne. "I know you will." She felt confident he could handle the stress and workload. "I want you to take leadership when I'm gone. I have faith that you can lead them to a better future. Keep Poison as your number one."

Brawler enjoyed the idea of it. He was hoping it wasn't the champagne talking. "I won't let you down." He paused a moment before adding, "I've always told you how I felt, and I've never once gone against your wishes. But I think this madness can't be accomplished."

Prestige finally broke down, "If it would make you feel better, let's send out some scouts to see if the Chronicles are near. You've served this family for years. You're very loyal, and it's time that you have your moment. I'm willing to put my plan on hold to send out scouts. In the meantime, the workers can rest for a bit. How does this make you feel?"

Brawler was quiet for a moment before agreeing, "You won't regret it. Once we're in the clear, I'll feel much better about you going to Mystic Cloud."

"And if they are up to something?" she asked.

He didn't want her to worry. "I'll take care of it."

Prestige tried to make him feel more comfortable and on board with her near-future plans: "The Chronicles no longer have Dr. Maximus to lead them. The only reason they got as far as they did was because of him. He told them about the Outpost. They have all the information they want on us. At this point there's no running. We have properties all over the country. That's our only saving grace. Maybe they won't know where to start."

Brawler wasn't sure. "Your guess is as good as mine."

Prestige was curious. "This got me thinking about Winston. Where is he anyway?"

"The last I saw him, he was with Poison and Polarize." He quickly added, "Rich and Kibosh might be with them, too."

"As long as he's kept busy," Prestige shot back.

Brawler suddenly sprang forward with an idea: "You and I want

Boswell gone just as much as the rest of the Revival. We've all risked losing something because of his arrogance."

She was eager to hear about it. "What's your plan?"

"If the scouts find the Chronicles close by, we can offer Boswell to them as a truce. They've been wanting to bring him to justice this whole time."

"Crescendo isn't stupid enough to fall for something like that."

Brawler nodded. "I agree, but it'll throw them off and give us a chance to strike first. It'll also buy you time to get to Mystic Cloud without the Chronicles on your back."

Prestige loved the way he thought. She perked up at the thought of it. "This could work." Prestige poured him a drink and handed it to him. "Drink with me, Brawler. You never cease to amaze me."

He clinked his glass of champagne to hers. "It'll work. Trust me."

Prestige asked, "Who are you thinking of sending?"

"If we just send out scouts, that should be simple enough. Do you have any ideas?"

Prestige suggested, "Send Rocco. He can shake his legs and show us what he's made of. Kibosh and Rocco were out on a job for the longest time. Now that they're back, be sure to keep them working. I don't want them falling asleep behind the wheel."

Brawler finished his drink. He would need to gather the men and switch them out in the fields searching for Gypsy Dust before moving on. While Prestige was obsessing over reaching Mystic Cloud, Brawler was focused on the thought of killing the Chronicles. With any luck they would both get what they wanted.

CHAPTER THREE

HEADQUARTERS

Sacramento, California. March 13th.

The workshop was loud as usual. Wrench kept himself busy all day fixing things and repairing vehicles for the team. He was a workaholic. Redford and Pike helped expand the workshop to give him more space to work. Everything was just the way he liked it. Wrench was feeling accomplished at the moment and decided to take a rare break. He sat down near the workstation, listening to his rock and roll music.

Greg Stewart had made his way into the garage to have a talk with him. Redford had already beaten him to the punch. Wrench watched Greg approach him, exhausted and overworked. He couldn't help but chuckle at him, "You going to make it, friend?"

Greg wiped his brow with a work rag. "I think so."

Wrench pointed to a chair alongside where Redford was sitting. "Take a load off. You'll feel better."

Greg sat down. Redford greeted him, "How are things out there?"

Greg shrugged his shoulders. "It's going."

She knew he was tired. "You seem off lately. What's on your mind?"

He played it off, "What do you mean?"

Wrench watched his dog Stooge wander through the garage. "Everybody seems to be on edge. I don't have to say what it's about. You already know."

Greg sighed, "I'd rather not talk about it."

Redford observed as Machine wandered the large garage, "Sometimes saying nothing is best."

Wrench yelled out to his dog, "Stooge! I need a beer!"

Stooge opened a mini-fridge and grabbed a beer and brought it to him. Greg was flabbergasted. "You've trained him for that?!"

Wrench opened his beer while Stooge sat at his feet. "I've trained him for many things."

Redford stood up and paced the workshop. "Have you guys noticed how Crescendo's parents are behaving?"

Wrench spat on the floor, "To hell with them. I know I should let it go, but I won't. Poor old Crescendo was expecting her parents to be great people. Instead, look at what she got."

Greg chimed in, "They might've started out as enemies, but now they know better."

Redford didn't care for them: "They're no good."

Greg disagreed, "Everyone has some good in them."

Wrench replied to Redford, "You and Fedora are very much alike. As nice as that man is, the two of you refuse to trust anyone unless they go through a line of questioning first."

Redford shot back, "What's wrong with being careful?"

Redford approached Machine and examined him for any scrapes

or rusted parts. "I hope you're listening to me and staying away from the hills, Machine. I can't afford to lose you. Crescendo, let you be my responsibility."

Machine stood still as she checked him over. "I've done as you've asked of me."

Wrench chugged his beer and tossed the can aside. "You're unaware of this machine, but you and I have been friends for a long time. The two of us, Redford and Fedora, would hang out back at Ghost Hill." She began to reminisce, "Those were the days. Back when we were all blind to what was truly happening in this world of ours."

Machine asked, "Did I like it there?"

"You had a bad habit of malfunctioning on us a lot. Half the time you were out," Wrench replied.

Greg reached up to rub his face. "I remember Homeland. What a nightmare trying to get out of there."

Redford wasn't in the mood. "Don't start."

Wrench nodded at the thought of it. "We all have our scars. There's no way around it."

Redford barked back, "That's the end of that for me."

"So, you say," Wrench shoots back at her.

Greg suddenly sprang to his feet and began pacing the length of the seating area. "I have something to tell you. I overheard Crescendo's mother talking earlier."

Redford nodded. "Constance. I hate her."

He ignored the comment, "Constance was talking to Raven about a strange feeling she was having. She said something about feeling uneasy about a sacrifice and that God was getting even with them. It was something like that. It was loud from where I was standing because of the construction being done downstairs, and Raven was agreeing he felt the same way. It could be nothing, or maybe it's something. I just felt I should tell someone."

Redford thought the obvious, "Maybe it has something to do with Mystic Cloud."

Greg wasn't sure. "It's hard to say."

Machine knelt over to reach out and pet Stooge. "Does Crescendo know the way you feel about Constance and Raven?"

Wrench gawked at him. "You sure are talkative today." Greg agreed with Machine: "We need to do the right thing and speak to Crescendo about this. After all, it does involve her parents."

Everyone stared at Redford. She took a step back, shaking her head. "Don't look at me."

Wrench explained, "You know her better. She'll listen to whatever you have to say."

"Crescendo will listen to anyone, and you know that! Besides, Hawthorne should be the one to do it. They're a couple now."

Wrench stood up and walked over to get a fresh beer. "He's her boyfriend now. Trust me, boyfriends don't enjoy bringing this kind of news to their girlfriends. Just go for us, Cinder."

Redford finally agreed, "Now isn't a good time. Crescendo and Hawthorne are having some issues. I'll need to wait it out. I'll have a talk with Crescendo the first chance I get." She then remembered what she needed to do. "That reminds me. Crescendo asked me to check on E.C.H.O. at the military base today. I'll speak with her later."

Wrench's demeanor changed. "Have fun with that. I'll never go down there."

Greg asked curiously, "Why's that?"

"The military base just brings back old memories. Boswell wasn't the only war I survived. I've seen my fair share to last two lifetimes."

Redford stepped outside the garage and stared into the sky. "I wonder what he's up to."

Wrench regretfully answered, "Boswell's doing what he does best: planning to destroy the world."

Redford turned to them, announcing, "We've done a lot of good here in California. Together we've made a stand, but I think it's time to move on."

Greg smirked, "You telling Crescendo that? Good luck. Her mind is set on staying here."

Wrench opened his beer and took a drink. "I knew it. Every time I get settled in, we need to uproot and leave again! I wish you people would make up your minds!"

Redford raised out her hands, calming him down. "I'm not the leader. You know that. Crescendo won't budge. Trust me."

Greg understood why: "We need to make a stand somewhere. The other places were falling apart and unsafe."

Wrench laughed, "Greg, sometimes you just have to take a chance!" He reached over to pet Stooge. "No wonder you and Hawthorne keep butting heads."

Greg was offended. "That's not very nice. I thought you and I were on the same page."

"Yes, I agree that Hawthorne can be strict, but chances need to be taken, or you'll miss out on the future. Imagine if Crescendo didn't want to travel outside of D.C.; none of this would've ever happened.

See what I mean?"

Redford smirked, "Well played, senile."

Greg made a note of it: "Since you put it that way." He paused a moment before adding, "It's still dangerous to go traveling around."

Wrench replied, "I know, but even you kicked into gear and made a move out of Homeland when Lockjaw was on your back."

Greg raised his hands, surrendering. "I get it, thank you."

Wrench swiftly added, "Now we're on the same page."

Greg grinned. He spaced out for a moment before opening up to them, "I remember the old days. The war began several years ago, but here I am talking like my past has been ancient history."

Wrench stopped petting Stooge. "Don't beat yourself up. I feel the same way. We all had our lives before Boswell was kind enough to slaughter millions of innocent people."

Redford started laughing. She took a moment to collect herself. "Weren't you a mechanic?!"

A sudden look of embarrassment came over Wrench. "Yes, it's true. So, not much has changed for me. I just remember having different customers instead of the same ones repeatedly."

Redford was lighthearted about it: "At least you're good at what you do, senile. We could never replace you as a mechanic or a friend."

He grinned. "I had my own shop and everything."

She nodded. "You told me about that."

Wrench carried on, "My father owned a shop in Wichita, Kansas. I had a younger brother that worked there with him. He wanted to start his own shop someday."

Redford chuckled, "Why not just start a family business like everyone else? Why did you part ways?"

Wrench laughed, "You don't know my family! They're impossible to get along with! Everyone wants to run the show!"

Greg wasn't surprised. "I saw that coming. Most families are that way."

Wrench jokingly added, "Most families have a history of law enforcement or military background. Mine was a family of mechanics."

Machine interrupted the conversation, "Why is everyone laughing at Wrench?"

Greg explained, "We're not laughing at him."

Wrench shrugged, "I guess Maximus forgot to install a sense of humor in Machine."

Redford stood up for him. "Machine's perfect the way he is." She turned to wave him away. "Go play with Stooge or something. We're talking."

Greg watched Machine turn and walk away with Stooge. "I remember when you guys had been trying to fix Machine."

Redford corrected her, "That was the old Machine you're thinking of. Maximus gave us the newer one before we left New York." She hung her head out of respect, "After he was killed."

Wrench felt like he should've treated Maximus better. "Not many of us gave him a chance. He felt a world of guilt for what he was forced to do. How do you come back from that?"

Redford spoke in his favor, "You don't." She remembered him for how he was: "I never really trusted him, but he had a lot to do with how Crescendo turned out. We owe him for that."

Greg agreed, "Amen."

Wrench thought about the enemy: "The Revival's days are numbered. The same for Boswell. They know it, too."

Greg thankfully nodded to Redford. "I don't know how many times you Chronicles saved us in Homeland. You must've been getting tired of us always needing your help."

Redford denied it. "Believe me, it was an honor to help. Crescendo felt like she didn't do enough. I remember she tried hunting using her orbs but only scared away the game. She had to learn to shoot just to get food for everyone in Homeland. She can actually shoot pretty well now."

Wrench smirked, "Hell, I can't shoot anything even at close range. I guess we don't need to worry about any of that anymore, though." He decided to share something with them: "My biggest fear was always death. I remember as a young man it bothered me something awful. As you get older you reflect on the choices you've made and the ones you've missed out on. Eventually death comes back around full circle. During the war I was lost and alone. All I had was Stooge for company. Just a stray dog." Wrench glanced at Redford. "That's when I met the Chronicles."

Greg sat there with a bewildered look on his face. "And what about death?"

A look of content came over him. "Now I'm not scared anymore." He quickly added, "My family wasn't as lucky as I am. After the war began, I saw my brother die right in front of me. I was separated from the others." He sighed heavily. "They didn't make it. There's just no way."

Greg opened his mouth as if he were ready to share his past with them. He lowered his head and left it at that. The memory of his wife was still a burden. Redford knew it was a problem. "No more of that. The war's taken enough lives."

Greg replied again, "Amen."

Wrench agreed, "Truer words haven't been spoken."

Redford pointed to Machine. "Stay with Machine for a minute. I'll be right back. I need to find Crescendo." She walked along the factory outside and followed a path to the parking lot and saw Jasmine speaking with Offspring near the new watchtower. Redford interrupted their conversation, "What's going on over here?"

Offspring still refused to take off her mask. She reached up to adjust it. "There's a possibility Boswell is near."

Jasmine stood with her hands on her hips. "Do you honestly believe it?"

Offspring promptly replied, "I wouldn't lie to you."

"I know that." Jasmine knew she needed to prepare everyone.

"I suggest you put your people on standby. If Boswell and his men really are about to attack, we need to be ready for him."

Jasmine nodded. "I saw that you were discussing this with Hawthorne earlier, too. How did he feel about it?"

Offspring didn't get personal, saying, "That's between the two of you."

She was appreciative. "Thank you for that."

Offspring wanted to be helpful: "Tell me what you need me to do."

Redford cut them off, trying to get Jasmine's attention. "Can I speak with you for a moment in private?"

Offspring stepped away to give them a moment. Jasmine shrugged her shoulders, staring into Redford's eyes, annoyed. "What's wrong? We were discussing something."

Redford came right out with it: "Earlier today, Greg came to me and Wrench, saying that he overheard your parents speaking and saying that they felt strange and uneasy about a sacrifice and that God was getting even with them. I'm not sure what the hell it means, but given their history, I would check on it right away if I were you."

Jasmine stood there quietly for a moment. She knew as a leader what she had to do: "Thank you for bringing this to my attention." They walked to the front gate at the beginning of the parking lot. "I can have E.C.H.O. put on standby while you come up with a plan." Jasmine was highly disappointed in her parents. "In the meantime, I'll have a word with Constance and Raven." She quickly added, "I know I'm asking for a lot, but try and keep this quiet for now. If everyone finds out what's going on, the civilians will lose their minds."

Redford agreed, "I'll pass the word on. Nobody will know a thing until you allow it. I just needed to get this to you right away."

Jasmine praised her, "No, you did the right thing. Thank you, Cinder." Jasmine stared off into the distance, saying, "Forget about going to the military base. E.C.H.O. will be fine over there. Stay here just in case I need you for anything." Redford nodded. Jasmine turned and headed back to the factory together. "I'll let you know how everything turns out with my parents."

CHAPTER FOUR

7:43 P.M.

There was a room on the first floor further in the back of the factory where Jasmine would have her daily meetings. After taking the time to pull in Constance and Raven to one side of the table, Jasmine sat with Redford, Kim, and Sinclair on the opposite side. Machine stood behind them near the wall. It was time for them to get to the bottom of the recent rumors.

Jasmine stared at her parents as they sat there quietly. "Thank you for meeting us here."

Sinclair wanted to know the news. "So, what's going on? Everyone appears to be off balance. Is there something going on with the Revival family?"

Jasmine told them, "It appears we might have a different problem on our hands."

Kim took note of how nervous Constance and Raven were. "What have you two done this time? Crescendo keeps giving you opportunities to change, but you refuse."

Constance hated the Chronicles. She was only there for her daughter. "The Revival family will find us eventually. They already know where we are."

Sinclair wasn't sure what to believe. "How do you know all this?"

Constance ignored him. "You're running out of time asking us these stupid questions. We haven't done anything wrong."

Sinclair reached up, placing his Tommy gun on the table. "You don't want to talk to me, huh?"

Redford crossed her arms, annoyed with them. "They don't want to talk to anyone."

Sinclair turned to Jasmine, "You going to put up with this?"

Redford sighed, "You people owe us. We've saved you more than once. This is how you repay us?"

Jasmine sided with her team: "They make a good argument."

Sinclair leaned forward, staring at Raven. "How about talking to us before we lose our patience?"

Raven lowered his head. "There's nothing you can do."

Sinclair agreed, "You're right, because you're not talking to us!"

Kim gave it a try: "Think of the innocent people here."

Constance took a deep breath and slowly exhaled, "Prestige is close."

Jasmine asked, "Is she on her way here?"

Raven tried getting Jasmine's attention. "You don't feel that Crescendo? You should feel what we're feeling. You're part of Mystic Cloud. You're part of us."

She shook her head repeatedly. "I feel nothing."

Raven educated her, "The Gypsy Dust has been discovered. It's only a matter of time now."

Constance stared across the table, locking eyes with her daughter. "The Gypsy Dust is from God. Prestige is after it."

Jasmine needed quick answers: "Why would she want Gypsy Dust, and what is it?"

Raven told her, "The possibilities are endless if you possess it."

"Why did it take so long for the Revival family to get to this Gypsy Dust? What is it anyway?"

Constance shouted, "If Prestige collected enough of it, she could return to Mystic Cloud and challenge God. That's what she's after. That's what she wanted for herself and her sister, the Tempest, before we killed her. Prestige's plans haven't changed."

Kim tried not to panic. "That doesn't sound good."

Sinclair asked the golden question, "We can stop Prestige, right?"

Raven adjusted himself in the chair. "That depends on how much of the Gypsy Dust she's already collected and where we are before she uses it."

Jasmine glared at her parents in frustration. "When the hell were you going to tell us all this?!"

Constance replied, "I just did." She felt no remorse.

Kim clutched onto her vial of Divinity. "God help us."

Raven agreed, "It would be nice to have His protection during these troubled times."

Sinclair wanted to make sure he was heard: "The only reason none of us have killed the two of you yet is because you're Jasmine's parents. Your arrogance isn't helping your case."

Kim nodded in agreement. "That's about the size of it."

Jasmine refused to disagree with her men. "Stop screwing around and tell us everything. What's she after?"

Constance answered, "She's after God's position. If Prestige can open a portal leading back to Mystic Cloud, she has a chance at defeating God. The whole world will be in her hands. Forget about Boswell. He was after the country. Prestige will take the world if she isn't stopped."

Kim thought it was crazy. "That's ridiculous. God can't be defeated."

Constance informed them, "He left behind Gypsey dust that had fallen from his hands as he created the world. Prestige will return to Mystic Cloud using His own powers against Him."

Sinclair took off his fedora, twirling it on his index finger. "How does this keep happening to us?" He leaned back in the chair, saying, "Let's not go too far with this. How's Prestige going to open the portal to Mystic Cloud with the Gypsy Dust? Someone please explain that to me. She would need something to make that possible."

Constance shut them down, "That's for you to figure out."

Kim didn't like the sound of it. "We need to stop her, but will there be enough time?"

Suddenly Divinity began to shine inside the vial around Kim's neck. Everyone watched and listened as she spoke calmly, "There is time."

Jasmine asked, "Divinity, what will happen if we don't make it in time?"

There was a short pause before she answered, "Mystic Cloud will be no more."

Sinclair put his fedora back on. "The usual news we get."

Divinity then added, "God has a way for you. Go to the Revival and stop them."

Redford wiped sweat from her brow. "This is insane."

Jasmine leaned forward to ask, "Divinity, will we make it in time if we leave now?"

Divinity replied, "Sacrifice is everything. There are two roads you can travel. No matter which road you choose, there will still be tragedy."

They stood there quietly trying to figure out what that meant. Jasmine asked, "Will everything be ok here at the headquarters?"

Everyone waited for the answer. Divinity spoke, "No. Choose what is most important. Sacrifice is the only way through this."

Jasmine kept at her, "Divinity, if we go to the Revival and stop Prestige, will the people of California survive?"

Divinity didn't reply. After a moment Sinclair leaned forward, grabbing his Tommy gun and standing. "We got our answer. Time to go to Texas."

Jasmine stood with a worried look in her eyes. She thought about the tragedy Divinity spoke about. Jasmine shook it from her mind and got back to work. "Remedy, it's time to get everyone together. We head out at first light. We're no longer facing Boswell but something much more dangerous than before." She paused a moment to take a breath. "Get everyone on alert."

March 14th.

For some people saying goodbye was difficult. Jasmine knew regardless of what she and the Chronicles did, there was a chance their world wouldn't be the same. She knew she couldn't save them all. Perhaps that was the lesson she needed to face. Hearing Divinity speak those words gave her a chill down her spine, but if there was an opportunity to put an end to the Revival family and Boswell once and for all, then it would be worth the sacrifice.

While the others gathered their things and loaded them into the vehicles, Jasmine took a minute to be with Hawthorne. The two of them sat on the ledge of the roof of the factory. They sat there quietly for what felt like an eternity. Hawthorne turned to Jasmine, grabbing hold of her hand. "You're making this difficult for me and my men."

"I'm pretty good at doing that lately," she regretfully replied.

He watched a nervous stare in her eyes. "You can do this."

She forced a smile on her face. "I'd rather you come with me."

"I can't. I need to stay behind to run E.C.H.O. They need me. The civilians need the protection."

She clutched his hand. "I need you too."

Hawthorne didn't have the proper words: "I'm not very good at goodbyes."

"I don't know anyone that is."

Hawthorne needed her to know the truth: "You're doing the right thing. You've always done the right thing. We need you to save us from the Revival family. I'm not capable of doing that. You are. This world is full of hate and evil. It's best to keep moving forward the way you've always been. Don't let their ways stop you from having yours. It's time to end this, Jasmine. Expose them all for what they are and take them down once and for all."

She sat there taking in his words, "I don't know how I was chosen for this."

Hawthorne told her, "It was by birth."

She turned to lock eyes with him, smiling. "You called me Jasmine."

Hawthorne stood up with her, and they slowly made their way back. "I'll be here when you get back. I always am." He reached out to take her by the hands and gently kiss her lips. "Love you. Watch your back out there."

She buried her head into his chest for a moment. She felt the safest when he was with her. Jasmine pulled herself away. "Love you, too."

Hawthorne didn't want her to leave broken-hearted. "Come back to me when this is over. This time it'll be the end of all our worries."

She forced a smile on her face. "Promise?"

He kissed her again before letting her go. "Promise."

THE REVIVAL

El Paso, Texas. March 15th.

The structure that held the Gypsy Dust wasn't far from the Revival's property. Towards the mountains there had been drilling into the ground in search of more of the material. Everything was going according to plan. Prestige waited at her mansion after sending out some of her men to have a look at the facility and the progress they were making.

Brawler brought his old comrades Poison and Kibosh along for the ride. As they pulled up to the property in their Hummer, they stepped out to stare at the marvel before them. Brawler approached one of the many large holes drilled into the earth, staring into it. "It makes you wonder what else we're capable of finding here. I know it's not just Gypsy Dust on this property."

Poison stood at his side glaring through his goggles. "It makes me wonder if Prestige is crazy or just damn well brilliant."

Brawler turned to him, asking, "You support what she's doing?"

"I support the Revival. No matter what insane ideas they come up with."

Brawler turned to Kibosh. "What do you think?"

She wasn't impressed after seeing what Boswell had built. "Does it matter?"

"I like to think that it does. You're on our side now." Brawler stepped away from her.

She was just honest: "I've seen bigger."

Brawler grinned. "I can see why Prestige approves of you." They followed him around the property. "Our men are gathering all the Gypsy Dust they can find. They're bringing it inside this facility to be held. I'll show you."

Kibosh didn't understand. "I don't understand why this is so important."

Brawler told her, "I wasn't sure myself until just recently. Prestige seems to think she can open a portal to Mystic Cloud using this shit."

Poison stared at containers that were lined up across the property. Inside the facility Gypsy Dust was colored gold and light brown. Kibosh smirks as she examines it all around the property and on the ground. "It sparkles."

Brawler nodded. "It's easier to spot that way."

Poison reached his hand across the ground to grab and study some of the Gypsy Dust. "How will this help her?"

Brawler walked towards the facility with them. "It's a long story. I'll explain everything in detail. For now, Prestige wants me to show you around so you can report back to her. She wants to know if everyone's working."

Kibosh was starting to think she made a mistake joining them. "She's crazy."

Brawler shook his head. "I'm sorry, what do you mean by that?"

"I'm an excellent judge of character, Brawler. I can see you feel the same way. I've learned that Prestige and Boswell are the same person. He was a madman that wanted to take over the country, but she wants the world. I'm still on your side. There's no crime in admitting your boss is crazy. All the greats are."

"Just as long as you're not part of our problem, you won't have anything to worry about. Trust me, this won't last too much longer."

"I've been hearing that for months."

Poison followed behind them, observing his surroundings. "This is impressive."

Brawler stepped up, opening the door to the facility and entering with them. "Here's where they bring the material." It was a large circular room. Brawler watched them walk around freely to examine everything. "This is what Prestige has been working on."

In the center of the room was what appeared to be a large reinforced Plexiglas tube that stood as tall as the facility. A control station stood alongside it. Poison reached out, shaking Brawler's hand, "Very impressive."

Brawler explained, "We're nearly there. Once we have enough Gypsy Dust collected, there are heavy-duty motorized fans underneath this container that will blow and mix the material together as it's pushed to the roof."

Kibosh stared at the machine and saw that it was nearly full. "You have enough, right?"

Brawler nodded. "That's right." He pointed to the ceiling. "When the Gypsy Dust has a chance to mix together, we'll open the rooftop just before turning on the system. Prestige believes this will be enough to open a portal when she's ready."

Poison asked, "How long is the portal expected to remain open?"

Kibosh nodded, "That's exactly what I was going to ask."

Brawler annoyingly answered, "I don't have all the answers. I just know what she told me."

Kibosh walked around the room. "Who built this for you? Dr. Maximus is no longer alive."

Brawler answered, "I know, but he left behind some rather talented friends that gave us a hand. They're nothing like him, but they got the job done."

Poison randomly asked Brawler, "What are you getting out of all this?"

"We go back a long way, Poison. Just say what's on your mind."

Poison faced him. "I remember you for how you used to be. Something changed over the years."

He barked back, "War changes people!"

"No, not this war. Something else was involved. I don't know what it is, but you're just not the same."

Brawler gave him a stern stare. "Are you wanting to go down this road with me?"

"Not at all. You know I respect you. I'm just more alert these days." Poison added, "I'm thinking after Boswell left for his war, he took a piece of the Revival family with him, even if we don't want to admit it."

Brawler understood what he meant: "You're thinking that has something to do with it."

Kibosh stopped and turned to watch them. "You guys aren't going to fight it out, are you?"

He smirked at her. "That's cute."

Poison shook his head. "No. Not with him."

Brawler moved on. He was pleased to see they could still work together and have their differences. "Now you can say you've seen Prestige's pride and joy." Brawler recovered from the disagreement with Poison and turned to Kibosh. "Prestige has allowed me to send out some scouts to make sure the Chronicles don't show up to interfere with her plans. If the Chronicles are heading this way, they can be stopped. I want you and Rocco to take some men and keep the Chronicles at bay."

Kibosh immediately agreed to the job, "No problem."

Brawler glared at her in confusion. "You're not at all worried? I like that."

She corrected him, "I'm worried, just not about the Chronicles." She headed for the exit. "I'm worried about the Strikers. Hendrix will be waiting for me."

Poison called out to her, "Kibosh!" She stopped and turned to him. He raised his right fist midway. "Be careful out there."

She gave them both a nod before turning to make her exit. "I'm coming back victorious." Brawler and Poison stood there quietly for a moment. They stepped further towards the center of the room, staring at the collected Gypsy Dust already poured into the large reinforced tube. The clock was ticking. Prestige would soon be ready to make her stand against God, Himself.

CHAPTER FIVE

Phoenix, Arizona. Six hours till destination.

Passing through the state of Arizona was no different than most of the country. Some level of destruction was bound to be seen regardless. The war left its mark even where it wasn't intended. The Revival family managed to have a hold on New York without firing a single shot. Redford followed behind the Harpoon in her Deathtrap through the state. As they got closer, the Chronicles felt nervous about the unknown. That was to be expected with what they were about to face.

Jasmine kept her eyes on the road but felt more and more uncomfortable having Constance sitting next to her. Kim sat in the back with Raven. Jasmine couldn't help confronting her mother: "I think it's sad I had to force the two of you to come along."

Constance stared out the window so she didn't need to make eye contact. "You're such a child." She shook her head appalled. "I had such high hopes for us to start a relationship. I always wanted you to forgive us and move past it. Even Boswell let us free to see you. That's what we wanted."

Jasmine: "Don't bring Boswell into this, and don't act innocent. God Himself didn't want you. There's no excuse for your behavior, not after everything we've done for you."

Constance turned to her. "Do you know why? You're bringing us to our fate as we speak."

Kim leaned forward, joining the conversation to set the record straight. "Divinity has told us to go to the Revival. It had nothing to do with Crescendo. If she's telling us to go there, it's a message from God as well. Perhaps there's something there you don't want to face, and you don't want to talk about it." They were quiet for a moment.

Jasmine shook her head, disappointed. "You're scared. You and Raven are good at running from problems. It's about time you face them for a change."

Constance confessed, "I know how this will end for us."

Jasmine barked back, "Let me guess, it ends with you answering for what you've done?"

Constance replied, "No, it's not just that. It also ends with the man you love getting slaughtered along with the rest of them in California."

Jasmine slammed on the brakes, causing Redford to abruptly stop the Deathtrap in a panic behind them. Jasmine turned to Constance, horrified with what she just heard. "What's going to happen?! Tell me now!"

Constance let out a heavy sigh. "Jasmine, you can't save us all."

"What do you mean?!" She frantically slammed her fist on the steering wheel, "Tell me what you mean!"

Kim didn't want Constance getting her upset. "Don't listen to her. She's just trying to get into your head."

Jasmine felt her heart sink. She sat there panting with her eyes closed. "Please, Remedy. Give me a minute."

Constance continued, "I know the true power of Divinity. She speaks the truth."

Jasmine kept her eyes closed. "What happens to Hawthorne?"

Constance regretfully tells her, "He dies."

Jasmine shook her head violently, unwilling to accept what she heard. "No, that's not true! It's not true!" She exited the Harpoon and walked out front for fresh air.

Constance stepped out to speak with her. "Please calm down. We can talk about this."

Jasmine ran her hands through her hair, pacing back and forth until she was able to calm herself. She demanded, "Tell me how you know this."

"Your father and I know what's about to happen. There isn't a way for you to win this."

"Explain!" she yelled.

"God speaks through Divinity. He knows what we're doing. He knows our progress. He knows all. When Divinity spoke to us back in California, it was a choice. You could stay behind and keep everyone safe or pursue the Revival family and Boswell to end the war. If you stayed behind, all would be well for you and Hawthorne, but the rest of us wouldn't be around to see it. The world would end." He gave her a moment to understand before adding, "Prestige wants to rule the world. We would be dead. You can't have it both ways."

Jasmine wiped her face of tears. "What will I accomplish going to the Revival?"

"When we arrive in Texas, you will be put to the test. God will give you a choice. He's allowed this to happen for the greater good. Your father and I face our own fate as well. We know what we must do. It is God's will."

Jasmine pointed to the vehicles. "Everyone I love dies if I choose wrong?!"

"No, that's not true." Constance reached out to hold Jasmine's hands and pulled her closer.

"This is the fight you've been groomed for. God is using you for His own reasons. Don't turn your back on Him the way your father and I have. Listen and obey your calling."

"All my life I was unwanted and left in the dark. Nobody loved me, and nobody noticed I was alive. You're telling me that somehow God has now decided to make something of me?"

Constance replied with a stern stare, "Yes."

"What happens to you and Raven after all this?"

She lowered her head. "I don't know."

"You have all the answers, but suddenly you're unsure of what will happen to the two of you?"

"We will know when our time has come."

Jasmine thought about Hawthorne, "I can't lose him."

"I'm sorry."

"It can't happen the way you say. There's got to be something I can do."

Constance replied, "I don't have all the answers."

Jasmine felt trapped, but even in the troubled times she still had hope: "I can make a way."

"There's always that possibility when it comes to God."

Jasmine sighed, "I just want this to be over."

"I know. So do I."

Jasmine nodded. "We need to keep moving."

"Do you want to take a minute to rest? You shouldn't push yourself."

"I don't know."

Constance felt her pain. "I know this is hard for you to hear, but we love you, Jasmine. Raven and I did what we could to save you."

"You sent me away to Dr. Maximus."

"It's all we could do." Constance felt terrible. "It wasn't safe to keep you with us."

"You could've done everyone a favor and not have given birth to me. It seems my life has brought so many questions and even more pain to myself and others around me."

Constance knew she didn't believe that: "You're just saying that right now because you don't think things will change."

"So now you know me?!"

Constance held back the tears. "I'd like to know you. Before our time is up, I'd like for us to be at peace with one another. All of us. Raven feels the same way."

"I forgave you two a long time ago for what has happened."

Constance felt blessed. "Nobody is ready for the obstacles they will face in life."

"Do you think I can turn this around?"

"I believe whatever happens, God has forgiven and provided a way and future for us all."

Jasmine was confused. "I don't know what will happen to everyone."

"There's only one way of finding that out."

Jasmine watched her mother go back to the Harpoon. Jasmine stood there for a moment before getting back inside. Kim reached forward, massaging Jasmine's shoulders. Jasmine let her know everything was fine. "Buckle up, Remedy. It won't be too much longer now."

Kim could see she was trying to get over it. She handled the pressure rather well, "You good?"

Jasmine nodded. "Yeah, I'm fine." She turned back onto the empty road. "We're making good time at least."

Kim tried helping her keep her mind occupied: "Did you want to take a break? I can take over if you like. It's not a problem."

"I'm fine. Really, don't worry about me. We've been through this before," she murmured under her breath, "many times."

Constance kept quiet. She thought it would be good if they didn't speak for a while. Kim just wanted to maintain the peace. "While you were outside, Divinity spoke to me."

Jasmine raised her eyebrows interested. "And?"

"We're on the right path. That's all she told me." Kim glanced over at Raven. "Isn't that right?"

Raven tried making conversation. "Yeah, it is." He shook his head in wonder. "How long has Divinity been with you?"

Kim proudly answered, "Long enough to know I can't live without her."

Raven shook his head repeatedly in awe at her existence. "Extraordinary."

Jasmine kept her eyes on the road. The surrounding area on either side was devoid of homes and businesses. Everything was reduced to rubble. Destruction was everywhere. On the right side of the road Jasmine had passed a destroyed playground at a kindergarten school.

She was saddened by the sight of it. "Did you see that, Remedy?"

Kim whispered a prayer for the children that had passed away, "Yes, I saw it." On the left side of the road, they passed a nearly demolished church. "I see this, too. What a time we live in."

Jasmine saw homes in the distance destroyed and abandoned vehicles on the side of the road. "It's almost not believable." She glanced in the rearview mirror at Raven. "Makes you question why this was allowed to go on like this."

Raven caught what she was getting at. "You know better than to say that. I would expect it from your friend Cinder, not from you."

Jasmine made her point clear but still defended herself: "I wouldn't dare say anything against God and His plans for us or this world. This is His world, not ours. I'm just simply saying that it's a shame we've fallen this low."

"I can see the changes the Chronicles and even E.C.H.O. have made. You're trying to fight against it. I know it's hard."

Jasmine barked back, "I don't need you agreeing with me." She was getting frustrated and began to stammer, "I, I just, don't." She took a deep breath, slowly exhaling to calm herself. She watched the road quietly nearly until her mind was clear before finishing her sentence, "I just don't understand why we're the only ones doing something." She sighed with exhaustion, "We can't be the only ones. I know that's not true. It's not possible."

Raven could feel her energy and the pressure she was under. "Crescendo, people aren't able to stand against the tyrants, monsters, and the evil of this world. Only a selected few are able to rise up to that occasion and make a difference. Not everyone is capable. That's why you're called heroes."

Kim watched Raven as he spoke. He didn't say much, but when he did, it came from the heart: "He's right."

Jasmine replied, "I don't know what to say anymore. I'm at that point. Does it really matter what we do or how far we go?"

Raven answered, "It does matter. A lot of people are counting on the Chronicles. You're the leader. It only works if you stay strong."

Jasmine was still frustrated. "Someone's always counting on me."

"Isn't that why you're here?" Raven asked.

Jasmine took a moment to rethink her words before remembering she was stronger and better than this: "I just get tired sometimes."

Kim immediately shot down the negativity. "We all get tired, but don't release those words from your mouth again, Crescendo! Like it or not, we make a difference in this world!" She pushed the back of the driver's seat. "You know better than that!"

Jasmine sat quietly for a moment, realizing that she had allowed herself to fall into despair. After pulling herself together, she smiled at Kim through the mirror. "Thanks, Remedy. I owe you one."

Kim was proud of herself. "That's why I'm here."

Jasmine glared at Raven in the backseat from the rearview mirror. "How are you holding up back there, Raven?"

"I'm fine, thank you." He locked eyes with her through the mirror.

Jasmine kept at him, "I've noticed you don't talk much. Not even to me. Why is that?"

Raven truthfully replied, "Because I know what we're facing: our sins."

"Can I ask you a personal question?"

"Of course." He waited to hear what she was going to say.

"Was it worth the sacrifice now that you know what's at stake?" Jasmine didn't want to pretend to understand what they were going through.

"For you, Crescendo, it was most definitely worth it. Ever since you were a baby, we knew the time would come. We knew one day you would learn the truth. We would take that as an opportunity to meet our daughter face-to-face for the first time. It was worth the sacrifice."

Jasmine felt their love and knew it was true. "You did that for me?"

Constance broke her silence. "It was supposed to happen this way. God isn't wondering what to do next. He's planned this. He's the Alpha and Omega. You're supposed to be here, Crescendo."

A sudden weight lifted from her shoulders. "I'm sorry."

"Don't be. We are the ones that are sorry."

Raven agreed with his wife, "Yes, we're the ones that are sorry. We've carried that with us, hoping to be forgiven by you." He was about to continue, but Jasmine cut him off.

"No, you don't understand."

Kim sat there trying to figure out what she meant. "What's wrong?"

Jasmine shocked Constance and Raven by confessing what's been on her mind: "I'm sorry we didn't have the time together." She held back the tears. "I wish we had time together." The vehicle began to swerve. She recovered and focused on the road. "It just would've been nice to have more time with you."

Constance knew she meant those words, "Thank you for that." She smiled. "We feel the same way." Constance took a long stare at Jasmine before turning away to shut her eyes. That feeling she had was what she had hoped for. To express her love for her daughter before the end.

THE REVIVAL

El Paso, Texas.

The mansion was dead calm. The soldiers were well on their way to California. Prestige was waiting for the last of the Gypsy Dust to be collected by her men. Everything was going according to plan. While she waited, Boswell was speaking with her in her room. Prestige was surprised they were on speaking terms since she had been overworking Boswell underground in the tunnels. She stared at him sitting across the room. "Are you afraid to sit next to me?"

He ignored her comment, "Are you ready for this?"

She watched as he struggled to keep his eyes open. "You've been having trouble sleeping."

"What do you care?"

She saw right through him. "I know how you feel about me, Winston. I know you hate me."

"Whatever gave you that idea?" he sarcastically replied.

She smirked, "You and I are the same person. We're both leaders. We've spoken about this before."

"That's true, and we even lead our men to be slaughtered. Congratulations to us. Haven't you learned your lesson yet? You're foolish enough to try to stand against them yet again?"

Prestige watched him sit there sweating from the brow. "The Chronicles are facing their own challenges right now. They won't be the trouble you're used to, Winston."

"You sent men out to California to finish off the rest of them, didn't you? You're trying to separate them from the Chronicles so it's easier to finish the job."

Prestige sat with a satisfied expression on her face. "It's rather genius. People are predictable."

Boswell watched her stare at him. He felt uneasy and suddenly suspicious. "You plan on having me killed, don't you?"

Prestige could see that he was nervous. "Brawler and Poison will be here with us. I've sent out Kibosh and Rocco to finish off the ones that get away. My work is almost complete."

Boswell noticed she didn't answer his question. He decided to pull back a bit with attitude: "I overheard Brawler and Poison speaking before about your plan." He couldn't believe how true her insanity really was: "You're crazy enough to challenge God Himself?"

Prestige crossed her legs, feeling confident in her chances. "I will beat him. When God is dead and gone, I will be the new ruler of this world and Mystic Cloud." She warned him, "And when that happens, I won't need the rest of you."

Boswell wasn't surprised. "Finally, you came out and said it. You'll have no reason to keep us around. I understand your ego's grown since I've been away."

"Don't give me any of your speeches or tell me that I'm wrong. You're Winston Boswell. You're known to be the most brutal, vile, violent, and insane tyrant this world has ever known. People don't know me the way they know you. I'm stronger than you, but you're the one with a reputation from hell. Because of you, millions of lives have been taken. You murder your own men just to prove a point. Don't lecture me."

Boswell laughed, "You're right! I'll shut up and let you walk straight into hell! What would you do if given the opportunity to rule? How far can you go until you're fulfilled?"

She sat forward, excited. "Now we're having a conversation. It's about time." She paused a moment before asking, "What do you think your parents would think of all this? Would they be proud of you?"

He doubted it. "It wouldn't be a pleasant conversation."

Prestige respected them very much regardless. "They did a lot of work for us. The family sought out only the very best. That was the beginning. We must keep the family safe."

The room went silent. Poison shockingly entered the room and stopped to glare at them. "Don't stop talking on my account."

Brawler cracked his knuckles while entering the room. "Rocco and Kibosh are ahead of schedule."

Prestige was pleased. "You see, Winston? Soon it will all be over."

Boswell stood up. "You're preparing to never have use for us again. I'll be around to witness it if you fail." He turned to point at Brawler. "Are you forgetting how this will be? Both of you need to get out of here before she brings down the wrath of God on the Revival."

Brawler was quiet for a moment. He didn't want to admit that Boswell was right. He reached out to grab him by the collar and pinned him to the wall. "You talk too much, Boswell."

Prestige turned to stare at them. "Get along, boys."

Brawler let Boswell go and stepped back. "Everything's fine."

Prestige prepared them for the final moments. "This is it, gentlemen. Brawler, take Winston to the Hummer out back." She reached out, placing her hands into Poison's. "You know what's about to happen here."

Poison nodded, "Don't worry about me."

She reached up to place her hand across his mask. "You poor soul.

You were born for greatness and cheated out of life." Prestige knew he was slowly dying from the overuse of his own chemicals. "You served us well."

He acknowledged her sign of respect. "I'm not denying my fate. People die. We all die."

She kissed his forehead. "And for you, death will come much faster, my dear."

Brawler pushed Boswell to the door. "Get moving!"

Prestige gave him a final look. "See you in the next life."

Brawler reached out to shake Poison's hand. "See you on the other side, comrade."

Poison quietly watched them leave the mansion. Prestige led the way outside to the back and entered the Hummer with the others. Poison watched from the window as they drove through the property to their next destination. When their driver started the engine, he shut the door and watched them head for their next destination. When he was finished, he made a quick exit out front. He turned on his jetpack and flew off into the distance to meet up with the rest of his men.

CHAPTER SIX

HEADQUARTERS

Sacramento, California.

Tensions were running high. Hawthorne sent his men to work with others around the facility to keep everyone calm. He was growing tired of the never-ending fight. Hawthorne decided to take some time away from the others and have a word with the few men that he trusted. He gathered Pike and Hendrix. The three of them went into their conference room for a talk. They needed to prepare themselves for what was coming.

Pike sat at the end of the table with his assault rifle resting alongside the chair next to him. He glared across the table at Hendrix, watching her chew her bubble gum. "Do you ever take anything seriously, Hendrix?"

She smiled at him. "This situation is serious enough. I'm trying to keep my mind off it."

The conference door opened, and Lockjaw entered. Hawthorne didn't approve, "What the hell are you doing here?!"

Pike pulled out a chair for him. "Let him stay. This concerns us all."

Lockjaw sat down. "I saw you three head over here. I knew

something was going on. Word travels fast. There's talk about Boswell coming for us."

Hawthorne: "We're trying to keep it quiet until we have a plan."

Pike agreed, "Start the meeting already."

Hawthorne sighed, "This is a rough time to lose every member of the Chronicles. We'll need to rely on the civilians' training and E.C.H.O."

Pike added, "We've got protection now. Things are different. There's enough of us to cover every side of the facility."

Hawthorne pointed outside. "We need to have some reinforcements at the barriers out front."

Hendrix joined in, "I and my girls can take them head-on in the front."

Hawthorne thought it over. "Keep Stamina with E.C.H.O. She's good with a gun. I'll have her in the back. The last thing we need is Boswell's men crawling up from behind."

Pike nodded. "Sounds simple enough. What about the roof?"

Hawthorne replied, "I'll have it covered. Some sharpshooters can pick off the enemy as they come marching in."

Lockjaw wanted to be involved. "You got a place for me?"

"What do you mean?" Hawthorne didn't want Lockjaw getting in the way.

Lockjaw got the picture: "I'm useful. You know I am."

Hawthorne leaned over, locking eyes with him. "Yeah, you are, but you also don't follow orders."

Hendrix suggested, "Perhaps he can take the rear with Stamina."

Pike didn't find any harm in it. "He'll be out of the way but still useful."

Hawthorne shook his head in frustration. "Lockjaw, you take the rear for Stamina. Try not to screw it up."

Hendrix felt better now that they had a plan, "I wonder how far along the Chronicles are."

Lockjaw stood up and headed for the door. "Don't worry about it. If there's anyone that has this taken care of, it's Crescendo." He opened the door and made his exit. "I'll be out here if you need me."

Hawthorne was tired of his company. "What did we do to deserve that guy?"

Hendrix shrugged her shoulders. "I'm not sure if you noticed, but there's something wrong with all of us here, not just Lockjaw."

Pike was shocked she stood up for him. "At least one of us is used to him."

Hawthorne waved his hand out to shut them up. "Look, Crescendo's not out on a picnic. Whatever the hell she's about to face is going to be serious. The same for us. Enough talking. Hendrix, get your girls in position." Hawthorne turned to Pike. "You and I need to find Harper, Heller, and Bergman. We'll be the first wave holding off Boswell's men." He clapped his hands together to get them moving. "Let's move out!"

El Paso, Texas.

Inside the facility, Prestige stood at the command center with Boswell at her side. Poison stood at a distance, observing them as they walked around the large container in the center of the room. It had been full of the goldish-brown Gypsy Dust. Prestige marveled at it. "It's so beautiful!" She turned to Boswell, pulling him closer. "Just look at it!"

"So, this is what you've been working on?"

Prestige was pleased with her accomplishments. "And to just think soon this magnificent piece of machinery will open a portal straight to Mystic Cloud."

Boswell watched her soak it up. "You think you'll survive going through it?"

"What makes you so doubtful?"

He knew she wouldn't make it. "God won't leave you with a leg to stand on."

"This very foundation we stand on was developed to assist the Gypsy Dust to keep the portal open longer. This will drain God of his powers, giving me the chance to overthrow him from his throne. It will work, Winston." Prestige turned to point to a guard near the command center. "Are you ready?"

Just as the guard gave her a nod, Brawler rushed inside the facility. "They're here!"

Boswell laughed, "That was short-lived!"

Prestige shouted to Poison, "Get out there and hold off the Chronicles!"

Poison rushed outside, joining Brawler. They stood out in front of the facility, staring at the Harpoon and the Deathtrap in the distance. Poison was surprised. "That's all they brought?"

Brawler cracked his knuckles. "Hell no. I'm not losing a fight to a handful of mutants." He rushed to a Hummer and jumped inside the passenger seat. The soldier behind the wheel started the engine. Brawler shouted to the other soldiers, "We're charging these bastards! Let's go! Poison remained at the entrance. He figured if the Chronicles got past Brawler, they would need to face him next.

The Harpoon was speeding in their direction with the Deathtrap at its side. Jasmine shouted to everyone, "Get your seatbelts on! "She kept the vehicle steady. Remedy, I'll need some of your magic on this one!"

Redford shouted from the Deathtrap's window, "Get the others to the Revival! We'll handle these guys!"

Kim shouted back to her, "What's the plan?!"

Redford pointed behind her in the bed of her truck, "Let's see what Machine can do! It's time he pulled his weight!"

Kim leaned forward to Jasmine. "Machine's about to get some exercise!"

Redford watched Jasmine speed out ahead of them. She turned to glance at Sinclair. "Hold on to your top hat, Fedora! It's about to get rough!"

He aimed his Tommy gun out the window. "We've been through worse than this."

Cross grabbed her assault rifle. "We need to buy Crescendo time!"

Inside the Harpoon, Jasmine got Kim's attention: "Remedy, wake up Divinity! Have her guide us through these goons!"

Kim grabbed hold of her vial, whispering, "Divinity, come forth and stop our attackers. Bless us, Lord. Keep us safe."

Jasmine continued speeding through the open field towards the enemy. She saw the Hummer with Brawler inside it swerve off out of harm's way. She shouted, "Remedy, now!"

Kim reached her hand out the window, throwing Divinity to the ground. A large force shield formed just as they passed the enemy. Two hummers crashed into both sides of the Harpoon's shield, causing them to drive out of control and flip over, crashing across the rough terrain.

Sinclair aimed his Tommy gun out the window, shouting, "Hit it,

Cinder!" Redford jerked the wheel, causing the Deathtrap to spin into a three-sixty while Sinclair opened fire with his tommy gun. Huge bursts of light shot all across the field, hitting several of the soldiers in the hummers. Redford regained control of the vehicle. Sinclair leaned out the window, shooting out the tires of one of the Hummers. It flipped forward several times before crashing.

Brawler shouted out to his men in the Hummers next to him, "Fire, fire! Kill these suckers!" The soldiers reached out their windows, shooting at the Deathtrap. Brawler sat back in his seat, "Don't lose them! Stay on them! They can't reach Prestige!"

Cross reached out the window with her assault rifle, taking aim, and drilled the driver with several rounds of lead. The passenger tried taking over the wheel but couldn't reach it in time. The Hummer skidded out, tipping over. Cross took cover from some return fire. "Do something about these guys! There are too many!"

Redford banged on the steering wheel. "Machine, get rid of them!"

Machine turned to face the hummers chasing them. His torso opened up, exposing a minigun on the inside. Machine's eyes turned red as he locked onto his targets. Suddenly the movements of the cylinders on the mini gun twirled as it opened fire. The front two hummers were turned into Swiss cheese and ignited into a large explosion across the field. Machine turned to give Redford the thumbs up. "I did it."

Redford laughed hysterically, "That's my boy, Machine!"

Another hummer came up on the side of the Deathtrap. Machine leaned out his arm, and it extended three times its normal length. Machine grabbed the driver from the vehicle and threw him in the air. The hummer lost control, losing their chance to stop the Chronicles. Machine watched another hummer speed towards them. One of the soldiers hung out the window with a rocket launcher. Cross shouted to Redford in a panic, "We have a problem, Cinder!"

Machine waited for the man to take aim. He fired the rocket just as Machine shot his fist at it, deflecting the attack. The rocket struck the ground, blowing the Hummer across the field. The impact blew the Deathtrap's rear end into the air. Redford regained control of the vehicle. Sinclair shouted out in a panic, "Speed up, Cinder! I'd rather not go through that again!"

Machine reached out his arm, and his fist retracted back into place. Another hummer came speeding towards the Deathtrap, trying to push them into the mountains. Machine extended his left hand, grabbing the axle, and with his right hand, he slammed it into the ground at full speed while pulling the vehicle, flipping it over the enemy. They crash-land onto the tires, regaining control. Redford rams into the Hummer, sending it into the mountain.

Brawler continued following the Deathtrap but couldn't believe they were still alive. He yelled to his driver, "We have to kill that Machine!" Brawler watched as Redford suddenly stopped to turn the Deathtrap around. Brawler told his driver, "Stop, stop!" He did as he was told. After a moment Brawler could see that Redford wanted to play chicken with him. He laughed at the humor of it. "You've got to be kidding me!"

The driver shook his head. "I'm not sure about this, sir."

He didn't care. "Punch it! Go! Ram them!"

The driver refused, "I'm not dying like this!"

Brawler reached out, grabbed the man, and broke his neck. He pushed his body out of the Hummer. "I'll do it myself!"

Redford stepped on the gas at the same time as Brawler. Sinclair buckled himself in. "You're not turning, are you, Cinder?!" She didn't answer. "Are you turning?!" She ignored him. "You're not turning!"

She shouted out, "You should know me better than that, Fedora!"

Brawler kept speeding towards them until he realized they weren't turning. "Die already!" As they got closer, he jumped out of the

Hummer, and the Deathtrap crashed straight through it. The Hummer flipped several times and landed off in the distance. Brawler got back on his feet after the crash and saw that the Deathtrap was destroyed and upside down. They were stuck inside. Brawler saw Cross crawling out of the back, reaching for a gun. He rushed over, kicking it across the field. "You've chosen the wrong side, Cross. You should've stayed with Kibosh."

She glared up at him, dazed from the wreckage. "Run while you still can."

He leaned down, grabbing her neck and squeezing it. "That's real cute. You die before your friends do." As she was choking, she reached out, pointing behind him. Brawler turned to see what it was. Machine punched him in the stomach so hard he flew across the ground several feet. Cross fell to the ground, recovering.

Machine pursued Brawler, "Execution mode: activate." As soon as Brawler stood up, Machine reached out his hands, grabbing Brawler by the arms. He pulled them downwards with full force, dislocating them, and kicked Brawler in the head, breaking his neck. Machine returned to the others to help them from the wreckage.

The facility had already been under fire. Jasmine and the others took cover after finishing off the last of the soldiers in the area. While they were in hiding, they could hear the machinery working inside the facility. Jasmine was getting nervous. "We have to stop Prestige!"

Constance reached out to grab hold of Jasmine's arm to get her attention. "If Prestige opens that portal, this will all be over! There's only one way to stop her!"

Kim ran to the group. "We're losing time!"

Jasmine ignored her and locked eyes with her mother. "What are you talking about?!"

Constance reached out to give her daughter a hug while whispering into her ear, "Give us time to make this right."

Jasmine pushed her away, asking, "What can you do to end this?"

A sudden look of purity came over Constance as she accepted her fate: "Sacrifice."

Raven reached over, giving Jasmine a hug. "We need to do this."

Constance told her the plan: "When we enter the portal with Prestige, it will all be over."

Raven could see that Jasmine wasn't able to process the information. "We must go now." He reached out, gently grabbing her face with both hands. "You will always be our little girl."

Jasmine was speechless and unable to fight it. They ran towards the facility. Kim held Jasmine back. "No, Crescendo. This is something they need to do."

Kim saw the fierce stare in her eyes. "We need to clear the way for them so they can get inside."

They turned and rushed towards the facility and saw Poison blocking the entrance. He called out to them, "Don't break any nails, ladies."

Jasmine ran with Kim side by side. Poison turned his jetpack on and flew towards them simultaneously. Kim fired Divinity in his direction. He dodged the attack and came down kicking them both to the ground. This gave Constance and Raven the chance they needed to slip inside the facility. When they entered, Raven lunged forward, punching Boswell unconscious. Constance ran to the control center and punched out the soldier. Raven pointed to the roof as the Gypsy Dust continued mixing and blowing in the large container. Raven shouted, "We're losing time!"

Prestige stood at the top of the stairs at the roof. Prestige saw them and knew she needed to move fast. Constance pointed across the room.

"There she is!"

Raven rushed over and followed Constance up the stairs. The portal to Mystic Cloud had suddenly opened as the Gypsy Dust continued to spin and blow through the facility and into the sky. Prestige spun around, yelling to Constance and Raven, "You're too late! When I go through this portal, I win!"

The sky began turning black, and the clouds shifted into a dark grey formation. Constance yelled as her voice became faint due to the heavy winds, "You will never understand, Mystic Cloud! Your time has come to an end, Prestige!" Wind violently blew across the field.

Raven shouted out, "We were all wrong to challenge God!" Thunder roared and lightning struck. Moments later there was rain falling and slashing the skin hard as it landed. Raven yelled again, "Sacrificing our lives for Him will cleanse us and end the Revival! It's over, Prestige!"

"Finally, we agree on something! It's over for you! I'm just getting started!" She was about to attack when Constance and Raven both jumped onto her. The three of them fell off the staircase and were caught up into the portal together. As the machinery continued pushing the Gypsy Dust, the portal remained open.

Outside, Jasmine formed several orange orbs in her hands, throwing them at Poison. He flew out of distance just in time as they ignited. The wailing sound of her powers caught him off guard. Kim took advantage of the opportunity and shot Poison in the chest with Divinity. He fell down, hitting the ground hard. Poison pushed himself back onto his feet, raising out his hands and shooting chemicals at them. As they covered their faces, he lunged forward, kicking Kim in the chest. He picked her up and threw her into Jasmine. They fell across the ground.

Poison watched them squirm on the ground. "I've been waiting for a fight! Don't disappoint me!" He ran forward, kicking Kim in the stomach. She rolled across the ground. Poison grabbed Jasmine by the hair and waist and threw her into the side of the facility. "Fight me already! You're the Chronicles!" He watched them try to recover from the hits. "So much for the chosen one."

Kim reached out about shooting him with Divinity. Poison kicked her arm away. "I'm not falling for that again!"

Jasmine got back on her feet and rushed over to help Kim up. "Let's shut this guy up."

He stepped aside, giving them space. "I'm waiting."

They stood up and ran towards Poison simultaneously. Jasmine threw her orbs out, forcing Poison to fly backwards on his jetpack. He landed and sprang forward, exchanging jabs and punches with the two of them. He kept dodging their attacks and making contact with them with punches to the face and rib shots. Seconds into the fight they were both down again. Poison stepped back. "You're beat. Give it up."

Kim remained on the ground. She pulled her attention to Jasmine. "I need to rest a minute."

Jasmine rubbed her back, comforting her. "Stay down. I'm tired of this guy." As she stood up, she formed one orb, dropping it across the ground. She faced Poison. "We're not through just yet."

He pursued her. "I was hoping you'd say that." The orb rolled between Poison's legs. He glanced down, being caught off guard. Jasmine sprang forward, kicking him in the chest with all her might just as the org exploded. The impact threw him into the hard structure of the facility, knocking him out.

Jasmine helped Kim to her feet. "Come on, we have to get inside and stop Prestige!" When they entered, they saw that the Gypsy Dust was dissolving quickly from being overused. The portal was beginning to close due to not having enough material. Kim ran to the controls trying to shut it off. "It won't stop!"

Jasmine looked up and saw Prestige, Constance, and Raven. She heard them yell out in pain. Their cries were heard through the noise of the machinery. At that moment she realized her parents sacrificed themselves to keep the world safe from total destruction. As the portal began to disappear, it crushed the three of them when it fully closed, killing them. Prestige's plans to rule Mystic Cloud had come to an end. The machinery began to spark and flame before breaking down completely.

The rain began to stop, and the sky suddenly returned to daylight. Jasmine stood there in awe as the portal opened for a second time. She waved Kim over to experience it with her own eyes. "Look at this! I thought it was supposed to close!"

The portal slowly moved out from the facility and stopped in the field. They exited the facility and watched the portal stop moving near the Harpoon. Just at that moment, Redford, Machine, Sinclair, and Cross were just making their way back to the facility. Kim pointed out to them, "There's the rest of them! They made it!"

Jasmine felt relieved. "Thank God."

The vial around Kim's neck fell off and dropped across the ground. It poured out, leaving a trail of water leading to the portal. The water began to form into a woman's figure. Divinity stood there still, made of shimmering light blue water. After the entire group was together, she spoke to them: "Come with me."

Jasmine stood in awe at the sight. "Come where?"

Divinity informed them, "You're needed elsewhere."

Redford stepped forward, asking, "Are we going to Mystic Cloud?"

Divinity answered, "Come with me and you will be shown what you must do."

Boswell suddenly stumbled out from inside the facility. He leaned against the wall, pointing to them, "No!" He yelled again, "Don't go through there! Boswell stepped outside, dropping to his knees. "Don't you go through there!"

Jasmine turned to him. "It's over, Boswell."

Sinclair stepped forward with his weapon. "I think it's far from over."

Divinity spoke to them again, "It's time to leave this place. Together."

Kim shook her head repeatedly. "We will follow you. We will."

Cross took that moment to reach out and shake Jasmine's hand. "It's obvious your work needs to continue. This is your show, Crescendo. Not mine."

Jasmine wasn't expecting that: "Come with us."

"No, you're the Chronicles. I have my own team. Perhaps someday we'll meet again." She reached out, aiming her assault rifle at Boswell. "Besides, I need to stay here and keep an eye on him. It'll give you time to leave. You never know what's up Boswell's sleeves."

Jasmine sincerely replied, "Thank you. For everything."

Sinclair reached out to shake Cross's hand. "It was a pleasure."

She smiled. "Give them hell, Fedora."

Boswell remained on his knees shouting, "No! Crescendo, stop!" He tried getting up, but Cross kept her assault rifle aimed at him. "Crescendo! Don't you dare go through that portal! I'm going to kill you! I'm going to kill all of you!" Jasmine entered the portal with her team. The portal disappeared. Cross stood there watching Boswell drop to the ground pouting, "You have no idea what you've done, Cross! You have no idea!"

She rather enjoyed watching him in that position as he was defeated yet again. "I've kept you from destroying any more lives. This journey was meant for the Chronicles. You're not standing in the way of that. Not this time." She turned and saw Poison slowly getting back on his feet. "The two of you will answer for what you've done."

Boswell stood up. "Nobody stops me!" He refused to accept defeat. "Nobody!"

MYSTIC CLOUD

The light shined across the stairs leading to where the pillars rested above. Jasmine and her team were kneeling as a pulsating beam of light spoke from the top of the stairs, "Here you are."

Redford, Sinclair, and Machine all bowed their heads. Kim tried taking a peek but only saw smoke forming across the stairs. "Show us what we must do."

Divinity stood near the stairs in the form of a woman. "Are you willing to follow?"

Jasmine was overwhelmed with the presence of God. "What is it we must do?"

The voice replied, "You must stop the destruction of my world."

Jasmine wasn't sure what he meant. "The world?!" She thought about her parents and the enemy. "What happened to Constance and Raven? What happened to Prestige? Didn't they save your world?"

He replied, "Their sacrifice saved the time you live in. Another time will soon need your help."

"What time? I don't understand."

He replied, "Divinity will guide you there."

Kim watched Divinity kneel to them, saying, "I will show you the way."

Kim was concerned for the others. "What will happen to the people here in our time?"

The voice answered, "They are safe."

Jasmine felt a weight lift from her shoulders knowing that Hawthorne and the others would live. "Where is this place we must go?"

He answered, "Go through the portal. You must find the Deserters. Together you must stop the Order."

"Who are the Deserters? What is the order?" She waited for an answer.

Divinity rose to her feet as God answered, "The Order has been taken over by evil. You must find the ones that refused their hand. Join them. Together you will fight again."

Sinclair kept his head bowed. He listened to what was being said but didn't fully understand how they would pull any of this off. Redford turned to watch as Jasmine took charge of the situation. "We will find the deserters. We won't fail."

The voice echoed, "Soon history will be changed. Soon others will come in their place."

Jasmine was trying to keep up. "What others?"

The voice said, "Find the truth and stop the evil."

Redford sighed, "More trouble."

Kim pulled her head up, glancing at Divinity. "We're ready."

The voice called out to them, "Stand." As the group rose to their feet, Divinity had joined them. They all turned to face the stairs as the light began to brighten to the point of blindness. Everything was calm for a moment. The voice then ordered, "Go, and finish this." The voice echoed.

CHAPTER SEVEN

THE ORDER

The Bronx, New York. June 12th, 2050.

Boswell stood in the conference room staring out the window at the city below. A slight grin of satisfaction came over him as he felt more empowered with each moment that passed. Boswell nodded at the sight of his accomplishments before hearing the conference door opening from behind. He greeted his guest, "Good afternoon. I trust everything is in order, Captain."

Pike shut the door before approaching the table to sit. "Why wouldn't it be?"

Boswell moved on. "And what about the help?"

Pike reached over to grab a glass of water and took a sip. "I was able to find some talented individuals."

Boswell was pleased. "And what about down below? Are your men finding it difficult to keep up with the workload?"

He leaned back in the chair, giving him the bad news: "We're soldiers. We're not slaves."

Boswell turned to him, explaining the importance of their situation.

"Captain, one day you and I will fully understand one another."

"I can see today isn't that day."

Boswell frowned with his witty comeback, "Are you trying to challenge me Captain?"

"Not at all. We just don't appreciate the treatment we've been getting. My men rely on me to give them what they need to survive. We can't be your muscle and slaves at the same time. Find someone else to dig your holes if you need it to be done."

Boswell pulled out a chair and sat down at the head of the table. "The Deserters were supposed to kneel to you, Captain. They were supposed to kneel to me most importantly. A couple of men working for you suddenly grew a conscience, bailing out on the Order and now standing against us. Before they left your command, they turned hundreds of others away from us when they could still be here working. We've fallen behind because we've lost these men."

Pike replied, "The Deserters are still running scared. You've ordered us to kill them on sight. I've only agreed because I hate them as much as you. The Order can only survive when we're all on the same page."

"It's nice to see that we're still together on this." He pointed to him. "But it was your responsibility to make sure nobody got cold feet. I need every man available to stand with us to complete my war. If I lack the support, everything will fall apart. I can't allow that."

Pike asked, "What do you expect me to do about it? I can't shoot every person I see just because they might be free thinkers."

Boswell disagreed, "Free thinkers are dangerous. Visionaries are dangerous. They both give hope. When you have hope, freedom will soon follow. I don't want them to feel they have the option."

"Aren't you a visionary?"

Boswell smirked, "Yes, but I'm an exception, and you know that, Captain."

Pike didn't argue with him. "Of course you are."

"Thank you for not disagreeing with me."

"Why would I? I tend to give my vote to the winner," Pike replied.

"And where are these little rats hiding these days? I'm starting to get annoyed with them. They seem to be growing in numbers."

Pike shrugged his shoulders. "It's hard to say. They're not easy to find. We were able to locate several of them the other night."

Boswell gave him his full attention. "Did they tell you anything useful?"

"Not at all. They're loyal. Just not to us."

"You still don't know where the others are hiding. Did you execute them?"

"Of course, we did," Pike replied.

Boswell was pleased. "Good. And where did you put the bodies?"

Pike took another sip of water before answering, "There was a ditch not far from where they were hiding. We buried them there."

Boswell leaned forward to give the captain his orders: "Dig them up."

"Sir?"

"Dig them up and put their bodies on display. I want the remaining deserters out there to know what happens when you stand against me."

"Yes, sir. I'll get some men on it right away."

"Good." Boswell was pleased.

Pike watched Boswell turn his chair around to stare out the window again. "Admiring your progress?"

"Why shouldn't I?"

Pike asked, "Are you sure you're ready for this?"

Boswell laughed, "Of course I am! In truth, it really doesn't matter how many deserters are left! At this point I can't be stopped!"

"You still have the aircraft to finish. The refueling station is nearly complete, but there's still work that needs to be done."

Boswell turned to him, announcing, "I have that covered. Dr. Maximus has proven to be very useful for me."

Pike thought it was brilliant how Boswell was managing everything even if he was still crazy. "How the hell did you get Dr. Maximus to cooperate with you?"

"Some of my men are holding his granddaughter hostage. To keep Dr. Maximus working, something needed to be done."

"And how does the Revival feel about this?"

Boswell slammed his fist across the table. "Damn them!" He reached up to wipe sweat from his brow. "The Revival didn't allow us to build in Queens. They don't want any part in this war, but that also means they won't get in my way. To hell with them anyway. You and the Order will back my play. When the war begins, the rest of this country will be left in shackles. The ones that live the good life are the ones that it was reserved for. There are too many people here."

Pike grinned, "In a perfect world."

"The weak have no chair at the table. I can live with that. So should you, captain."

Pike informed him, "The professionals I've located will be helpful."

"Let's hope they're up to the task."

Pike wanted to make him a believer: "They won't let us down."

"Are they better than your soldiers?"

Pike took offense to the question, "My men are ready to die for me."

"I'm not asking them to die for you. I'm asking them to die for me."

Pike pushed the water across the table. "They're willing to fight to the end. You should be grateful for that. While others are running away, most of my men stayed behind to help your war. Your own family won't even help you. The Revival wants nothing to do with this. Show my men some respect."

"My parents worked hard for the Revival. To them, I'll never fill their shoes. Do you know what it feels like to be told you'll never live up to someone?"

"So, this is why you're starting a war? Is it out of spite?" Pike asked.

Boswell smirked, "No, I'm starting the war because it needs to be done. It should've been done years ago."

"You must've gotten tired of seeing the scraps being fed to the dogs. I agree with keeping the rich in power, but remember it was the dogs and the weak that made this possible for us."

Boswell gave him a stern stare. "You feel sorry for them?"

"I'm only remembering how we got here. I'm remembering how this world began. At one point we all had nothing."

Boswell sighed with exhaustion, "We're all merely mortals in a world created by a visionary much like myself."

Pike found his arrogance to be intoxicating. "So, you think you're God?"

Boswell rubbed his hands together. "God can be questioned. I can't be." He pointed to Pike again. "I'm not as bad as many believe me to be. Like you said, we all begin with nothing. We're all the same in this world. We all come from the same source. It's only a matter of time before someone evolves to accomplish the goals that were set into motion before this world even existed. I just beat everyone to the punch."

"Just tell me where to shoot. That's all I'm here for." Pike was a true soldier.

Boswell nodded with approval. "Well said, Captain." He interlocked his hands. "So, tell me about your friends."

"What do you want to know?"

"How professional are they?" Boswell was hoping for only the very best help.

Pike didn't understand the question, "What do you mean?"

"After your men put the dead deserters on display, I want you to take your crew and track down every member they can find and kill them. Kill as many of them as humanly possible." Boswell salivated at the thought of it.

"The Deserters have women and children too."

Boswell showed no concern. "So, what's the problem?"

Pike drew the line: "We don't kill women and children."

"And yet you're still willing to serve me. You know I'm willing to slaughter millions without mercy. That would include women and children. Just get the job done."

Pike told him, "I'm not the one willing to do the murdering of women and children. That's on you. I'll be your protection on board the Kingdom, but that's as far as it goes from there."

Boswell couldn't wait to have his aircraft flying. "We will ride together. In the meantime, I don't give a shit about your morals, Captain. I'm giving you a direct order. Send your men to hunt down and kill every deserter they find. When Dr. Maximus tells us it's time to fly, it'll be the first step forward to a long journey. Nobody will stand in my way."

Pike didn't feel comfortable with the order but needed to follow it. "Yes, sir."

"Now tell me who you hired. Is there anyone I might've heard of?"

Pike answered, "Poison caught wind of this war. Do you think he'll be a problem for us?"

"Why would he be?"

Pike mentioned, "Because he works for the Revival family. His old comrade Brawler is now working for you. I thought it would be a problem, but I guess I was wrong."

Boswell smiled. "You've heard about Brawler?"

"It's my job to stay on top of these things." Pike had been involved with Boswell and the Revival for years.

"Poison is very much welcomed to climb aboard just as long as he's not bringing anyone else with him." Boswell respected the two of them: "Brawler and Poison is where it stops."

"They have a history. I've hired two new members, and they'll be here in a few days. Dallas and Trinity have made names for themselves. You won't be disappointed."

Boswell was curious, "You hired only two?"

"No." He paused a moment before telling him the rest, "Back when

I worked as a bounty hunter I came across some women that saved my life. I heard they were in the area, and they've agreed to meet with me." Pike wanted him to be at ease. "They're good. They call themselves the Strikers."

Boswell wasn't convinced yet. "And you trust them?"

"I do. They're worth the time and money." He was hoping Boswell would get on board.

"What are their names?"

Pike answered, "Victoria Hendrix runs the crew. There's Cross, Kibosh, and Stamina." He reached for the water and drank some more. "They're highly respected here in New York. I thought you'd like to hear that."

He swiftly asked, "They don't have ties with the Revival, do they?"

"Not at all."

Boswell didn't want any more members from in-house. "Good. Why haven't I heard of the Strikers?"

"I don't have all the answers," Pike sighed. Sometimes there was no pleasing Boswell: "They don't exactly advertise. I just got lucky running into them."

Boswell stood up and began pacing the conference room. "Captain, am I making a mistake leaving you in charge of the muscle?"

He wasn't shocked he asked that question, "Are you losing faith in me?"

"I just want to know if your heart and mind are in this till the end. Can I trust you to go to the lengths I'm prepared to push you?"

Pike stood and approached the window to stare at the construction being worked on below. "I've found you professionals. When you meet them, you'll be pleased. And to answer your question, yes, I'm prepared."

Boswell stood next to him, staring outside. "Soon it'll begin."

Pike was up to a difficult task. "It took a while to clear everyone out of the city. Now it belongs to you and the Order."

"The only people in the Bronx are the Order and the Deserters. I trust you'll locate their hideout soon. I know they must have many. There are endless places for them to hide."

"Are you thinking they'll become a serious threat? They haven't done much against us. They just don't want to be involved in the war."

Boswell was full of hate and bitterness: "They fled from us. That's a problem. Soon they will want blood. I've seen it before."

"Most of the people in hiding are soldiers. This won't be easy. I've trained a lot of them myself. They know how we operate, and they know what to do to stay alive. They'll help any others they meet along the way." Pike knew it was going to be like finding a needle in a haystack.

Boswell was getting frustrated. "That's why we must stop them any way we can!"

Pike kept him calm, "I'll take care of it."

Boswell turned to sit back down at the table. "In the meantime, I'll continue to have Dr. Maximus working on the Kingdom."

Pike followed behind him and stopped to lean against the table. "I wouldn't push that man."

"Are you getting soft on me?"

"Not at all, I just know what happens to people when they feel trapped." Pike warned him about that in the past before.

Boswell disagreed, "Nonsense. We have his granddaughter. He

won't do anything stupid."

"Fine, but let's talk about something else. This compound we're working on is in the heart of the Bronx. This very building stands in the center of our progress."

"What's your point?!" Boswell barked back.

"Do you think the Deserters might try attacking us here?"

Boswell thought about it for a moment. "It's not likely to happen, but if this building is altered or the compound in any way, it'll bring my plans to a halt. It's your job to make sure that doesn't happen."

"I'll put a twenty-four-hour alert on this facility and the compound. We don't have enough men to watch the Bronx, but I can have my soldiers brought here immediately. If the Deserters are planning an attack, they'll never make it to the front gates."

Boswell stood up to shake his hand. "You see, now you're a true Captain. I knew you'd come around. We all question ourselves at times. Even the best of us."

Pike stared at him. "Can I ask you something, sir?"

Boswell gave him his full attention. "Please do."

"Why'd you pick me?"

Boswell smirked, "Are you referring to my picking you to use your services? Or perhaps it's because I've invited you to board the Kingdom."

Pike replied, "You know what I mean."

Boswell was as open as anyone could get: "I see potential in you. I always have. When I look at you, I see a man that deserves to be part of the new world. A fighter. Someone to depend on and who knows his limits, only to push himself even further." Boswell abruptly stopped to lock eyes with him before adding, "You also have access to hundreds of soldiers that could serve me well in my war. Don't feel used even if you are. Remember, you're at the helm with me. That's a fair trade."

Pike wasn't offended. "I figured it was something like that. You know I had to go through hell to take command of those men. I don't know how you and the Revival pulled it off, but somehow the cards fall your way every time."

"Mind control. The entire state is under the Revival's thumb. It's useless to fight them. Even what's left of the military has been divided in some way and frightened with the idea of a war starting. They leave the Revival family alone because it could get worse."

Pike asked, "And what about the President?"

Boswell laughed. "What President?!" He pointed to himself. "When this war is over, that might be a position best run by yours truly!"

Pike was sickened by his arrogance. "You've got to be kidding."

Boswell seemed surprised. "You don't believe I'd make a good leader?"

Pike didn't deny it. "You make a fine leader. It's not easy to orchestrate your own personal war, but running a country is something different."

"When I'm through with America, it won't be a country anymore, not until I place myself in the seat and start fresh. I'll rebuild what I've destroyed. The millions that have been killed will leave plenty of room for my future plans."

Pike replied truthfully, "Sometimes I think you're insane, sir."

Boswell reached up to straighten his tie. "Thank you." He took it as a compliment.

"Why exactly are you doing this? It can't be that important to prove yourself out of spite. The Revival knows you're a talented leader. You don't need to live up to your parents' name."

Boswell confessed, "At first my thinking began that way, but things are different. If one man can start his own war, what else can that man be capable of? It's not about ruling the country for me. It's about the drive and how far I can go without being stopped."

"I try not to question you, but you'll need to elaborate on that, sir."

Boswell obliged, "Think of it this way. God had Adam name every animal in the Garden of Eden. How would you feel if you had the power to destroy, recreate, and mold things that had already been made complete by God, Himself? The country would become a blank canvas waiting for your visions to come to life."

"So, you're playing God. How long do you think this roleplay will last?"

Boswell was disappointed in him. "Much longer than you think. Do you see any heroes lined up to stop me?"

"All I see is the Revival family making sure your boat stays afloat while you have fun tearing the country apart. If everything goes south, the family will help clean up your mess, and the government won't get involved because they're in la-la land and under the Revival's control."

Boswell smiled, "Precisely!"

"You people certainly are ambitious."

"The Revival family has been thriving longer than most realize." Boswell was proud to be part of them.

"When does it ever end?"

"Why should it?" Boswell shot back.

Pike chuckled, "Even you know there's a time to end, a time to die."

"Perhaps, but not my work. There will always be someone to pass it on," Boswell added. "The Revival isn't going anywhere. You can be part of my plans or against them. The choice is yours, Captain. I never expected for you to feel uneasy about the matter. You used to be adamant about the matter. Please don't tell me you've changed or found religion."

"Please forgive me. I'm still on board."

Boswell reached out, grabbing hold of Pike's shoulders, staring at him. "You're overworked and overwhelmed. I understand that. I'm expecting a lot from you in very little time. This will pay off for us all. Trust me. This conversation never happened. I'm more satisfied than offended. A man that asks questions shows his true support and interests. If you were to ask nothing at all, things would've been different for you." Boswell stepped away from him.

Pike sighed, "I guess there's nothing else to say."

Boswell stared down at the city below through the window. "Take care of priorities before they take care of you, Captain."

Pike stepped forward, saying, "Excuse me?"

Boswell turned to him with his hands interlocked. "Take care of your priorities. If the Deserters get an open invitation to fight back, they're aiming at you first. Take them out before they have that chance, Captain."

Pike wasn't looking forward to it. "You're right."

"Innocent people die in war. Don't think about it. Just get the job done. This is the last time I'm discussing the matter with you, understand? Kill the deserters. All of them. Their families too."

"I'll report back after we dig up those bodies." Pike turned and exited the conference room, leaving Boswell there with his thoughts.

Pike turned the corner and walked down a long corridor to an elevator. When the door opened, Offspring stood there. She stepped out, greeting him, "Have you seen the big bad wolf?"

Pike let out a heavy sigh. "He's given me orders to locate the Deserters."

Offspring turned to walk to a seating area near the elevators. After they sat down, Offspring crossed her legs, leaning back comfortably. "They haven't given you too much trouble. They're running scared right now."

"I realize that."

She asked, "How does it feel to have your own men abandon you?"

"Not good. Why, do you have any ideas how I can get them back?"

Offspring stared at him through her mask. "That's not my line of work."

He leaned forward. "Remind me why you're here again."

"I'm here for the same reasons you are. Boswell has asked me to tag along on the Kingdom."

Pike pointed to her. "What makes you so valuable?"

"Are we ever going to get along, Captain?" She sighed, "Your ego will get in the way."

"I'm just trying to understand." He leaned back in his chair. They were quiet for the moment before he added, "I heard a project has been in the works. Dr. Maximus has his hands in everything these days."

Offspring asked, "What about it?"

"I heard Boswell sacrificed some important men to create some sort of a high-tech soldier. I wasn't sure if it was a rumor or not." Pike raised his eyebrows. "Who knows with him?"

"Why are you telling me this?" She waited for an answer.

"I'm sorry. My mind's all over the place these days. So much is going on." He was becoming overwhelmed.

Offspring reminded him, "Your concern should be hunting the Deserters."

Pike sighed, "Right. I'm supposed to kill the Deserters. That's only one problem. Boswell's expecting me to kill their families, too."

Offspring calmly replied, "It appears you have a choice to make. If you don't kill them, you'll answer to Boswell. If you follow through with your orders, all is well. If this mission of yours holds up the progress of the Kingdom, I would suggest you seal the deal quickly."

Pike was hoping for a different response. "I was afraid of that, but perhaps you're right." He stared at her, surprised with how calm she was. "What turned you into the person you are?"

"Life has strange ways of burning us when we least expect it. I'm numb to the pain." Offspring reached up, placing her hair into a ponytail. "Is Boswell busy at the moment?"

"He's still in the conference room if you need to see him."

She rose to her feet. "I'm sure we'll run into each other again, Captain."

Pike stood up to shake her hand. "I'm not a hard man to find."

Offspring turned and walked away, saying, "Good luck getting the Strikers to join."

Pike didn't understand how she got that information. "How did you know about that?!"

She turned the corner down the corridor. "Be careful with Hendrix! She can be a handful!" After taking a moment to gather his thoughts, he returned back to the elevator. He needed to take care of the Deserters before Boswell took care of him.

Offspring reached the office and entered without knocking. She saw Boswell staring out the window. "Every time I see you, you're in the same position. Have you been admiring your work all day?"

Boswell turned to Offspring, waving her over to join him. "Look at that beauty. Maximus has done himself proud."

Offspring gave him a quick jab: "People tend to work at their best when you're holding their family hostage."

"An attempt at humor? Sounds like you've been spending time with Pike." He seemed displeased.

Offspring watched the people working on the Kingdom below in the city. "I just passed Pike in the hallway."

"And what did he have to say to you? Or are you leaving that for yourself?"

Offspring turned away from the window and sat at the table. "We spoke about the Kingdom. He said he's looking forward to seeing it airborne."

Boswell sat at the table across from her. He studied her eyes. "You're lying."

"Perhaps I am. What Pike and I discuss is of no business of yours. Don't worry, he's not getting cold feet."

Boswell bowed his head to her, "And I assume you're still on board."

She was insulted that he was actually concerned. "Of course."

"The people in my life have become divided. Half want to see me succeed and the other half wants to see me fail." Boswell sighed, "That's why I've selected only a few to remain at my side."

"Go on." She readjusted herself on the chair.

"From the moment we attack, it won't be long before we're branded terrorists. The best part is there's no military to stop us if we have a rainy day."

Offspring stated, "I heard you pushed back the date on this. I'm guessing you had second thoughts about this whole thing. Am I right?"

"You're wrong. I pushed back the date to make sure everything was in order. Now that we're nearly there, history is about to be made." Boswell knew he could count on her. "You can stomach this kind of life. Pike is a good man but easily led astray. I'll need to keep an eye on him. I hope he reaches his full potential soon."

Offspring spoke up for him, "He'll be fine. All of us will be." She then asked, "And what about the other passengers?"

"What about them?"

"How do you select the passengers? Is there a list you follow?" She waited for an answer.

He explained, "Many of the passengers are members of the Revival family. They didn't want to be involved, but their immediate family members that aren't in any positions have asked to tag along. Naturally, I allowed it. As for the rest of the passengers, they're from the wealthy areas of California, some cities here in New York, and across Arizona and Texas too."

Offspring asked, "Do you pick them up?"

"Nonsense, they drive to this location. There's a refueling station already built in California. A second one will be built here in New York. The only times the aircrafts land are to be refueled. If the passengers aren't here on time, we board the Kingdom and leave them behind."

Offspring glared at Boswell through her mask. "How do you select the property? I was always curious how you go about doing that."

He waved his index finger at her with a mischievous grin. "Nice try. That's of no concern of yours. You're well informed. You and Pike really do spend a lot of time together."

She let it go: "Keep it to yourself." Her demeanor came off as annoyed.

Boswell changed the subject. "Besides, you should be more concerned about other things. I suggest you finish up any last-minute pressing appointments before we leave. Maximus is nearly finished, and I'm not waiting for anyone to get here on time."

Offspring nodded. "I understand. Before I leave, I did want to have a word with you about something."

Boswell glanced at his wristwatch. "It's getting late. Perhaps another time." He rose to his feet. "If you're concerned about anything relating to the Kingdom, don't be. If you need something to fill in your spare time, join Pike and his men. They're hunting deserters. Give them a hand." Offspring was about to reply when Boswell turned away from her and returned to the window. It was clear he wanted to be left alone. She quietly left the room.

CHAPTER EIGHT

Meanwhile.

The portal had already come and gone. Jasmine and the others had found themselves lost in a city with no people around. They kept their guard up as they explored their new surroundings. Everything around them appeared to be destroyed and abandoned. After realizing they couldn't locate any civilians in the area, they were about to search elsewhere until Divinity spoke to them.

Jasmine turned to Kim as Divinity told them, "You are close."

Kim gasped in relief, "How close?"

Sinclair tapped Machine across the chest. "You're taller than us. Do you see anything?"

Machine scanned the area for them. After a moment he gave them an update: "I'm picking up some body temperatures up ahead."

Sinclair snapped his fingers. "Bingo."

Divinity spoke to them again, "Follow the path."

Redford stepped out in front of everyone. "I'll take the lead. Give you a break, Crescendo."

Jasmine allowed her to lead, "Why should you have all the fun now?"

Redford smirked. She shoved Kim away playfully. "Let's go. We're wasting time."

Machine followed behind Redford. As they pressed on, Kim was trying to make a connection of where they were. "Anyone recognize this place?"

Sinclair kept watch in the rear. "Not unless it's Chicago."

Redford led the group. "It's hard to tell. Everything looks the same to me now."

Jasmine snickered at the comment, "I second that."

Machine told them, "Much of what I'm picking up are just rodents. Huge rodents." As he said that, several rats scattered the area.

Sinclair adjusted his fedora. "Really? Maybe we are in Chicago."

Jasmine tried making sense of it all. "Everything appears to look the same as before. Perhaps we were sent to another year, and this is New York."

Sinclair added, "Or perhaps Chicago. They look similar."

Redford smirked, "That's right. I forgot you were from Chicago."

Suddenly Divinity began to shimmer. "Stop where you are."

They stood there quietly until they heard some noises coming from ahead. Jasmine prepared herself by forming orange orbs in the palms of her hands. Suddenly a greyhound ran towards them from behind some rubble, barking repeatedly. Jasmine dropped her defense, choked beyond belief, "Stooge?!"

Sinclair couldn't believe it. "Did you say Stooge?!"

Redford knelt over to pet him. "Stooge?! How are you doing, boy?!"

The dog continued barking just as it turned away from them and ran ahead. Jasmine yelled out, "Come on! He wants us to follow him!"

They took off after him towards a path that they would've never found on their own. One by one they slid down some wreckage near a row of demolished buildings. They dropped down into a hidden area under the street. Jasmine took the lead, going first, and waited for the others to follow. She realized the group had separated somehow. "Where are Fedora and Machine?"

Redford told her, "Fedora stayed behind. Machine couldn't fit through."

Kim scanned the room just ahead. It was dark and muggy. "Did anyone see where Stooge went?" They stepped through a pathway that had been premade.

Jasmine dusted herself off, coughing from the poor air quality down there. "Keep your guard up. There's no telling what's ahead."

Further in the distance they could hear Stooge barking. Redford raced out in front. "Let's go!"

They followed her into the next room. The space spread out into a large open room full of seating and sleeping areas and more. Two men entered the room from another entrance. They were dressed like soldiers. Their uniforms were the very same uniforms of Captain Pike's men. Jasmine stepped forward with caution, asking, "Who are you?" They didn't appear to be a threat.

The first man stood there stroking his goatee, studying their guests. He had brown hair and brown eyes, was fit and of average height, and appeared to be in his late thirties. He raised his hand, showing them, he meant no harm. "My name's Jericho."

The second man had brown hair and green eyes and appeared to be in his late thirties. He was also very fit and above average height. He reached out to shake Jasmine's hand. "You'll have to excuse my brother, Jericho. He's straight to the point. Call me Gabriel." He could see they were questioning the situation. "We've been expecting you."

Jasmine had so many questions: "How were you expecting us? What is this place?"

Gabriel answered, "This might take a while to explain. Let's step into the next room and talk."

Redford mentioned, "We followed a dog here! Where is he?!"

Gabriel whistled for the dog. It ran into the room and stopped at Redford's feet so she could pet him. Gabriel smiled. "He likes you. It's usually afraid to approach people. There's so much shooting around these parts. Everyone's in hiding."

Redford gave Stooge some much-needed attention. "Of course, this dog likes me!"

Kim asked Gabriel, "Everyone's in hiding?"

"Yeah, times are challenging."

Redford was happy to see Stooge again. "Wait awhile. It gets much worse."

Jasmine pointed to the dog. "Where did you find him?"

Gabriel answered every question they had, "He found us, actually. It was about two months ago. He was resting next to a dead guy. He wouldn't leave his side." He quickly added, "Do you know the dog?"

"His name is Stooge." Jasmine lowered her head out of respect for the dead. "We called the owner Wrench. It was his dog." Jasmine figured Wrench was killed before they could save him from the past, or perhaps the dead man wasn't him at all. They would need to wait and see.

Kim held back some tears. "He's in a better place. How did he die?"

Gabriel shook his head. "I'm not sure, really. We just found the dog there. It came with us."

Jericho interrupted, "Let's move on. The others are waiting."

Gabriel nodded. "You're right." He asked Jasmine, "You have more men with you, right?"

"They're above us. By the way, I'm Crescendo." The others introduced themselves as well.

Jericho waved his hands at them. "Now that we got that over with, we need to move on."

Jasmine and the others followed the two brothers through the hideout. Gabriel continued talking to them along the way, "We didn't expect you so soon."

Jasmine remained close. "What do you mean by that?"

"We prayed and hoped for a brighter future. We were told God would send us warriors."

Redford found it hard to believe. "You knew we were coming?"

Gabriel nodded. "You were in Mystic Cloud, right? That's how we knew you'd be here. To help us bring an end to the Order and Boswell."

Jasmine was shocked hearing that name being mentioned. "Did you say Boswell?"

Jericho helped his brother out. "That's right, but God sent you, so everything should be fine," he sarcastically replied.

Kim asked, "Are you two part of the Deserters?"

Gabriel tried to fill them in the best he could. "That's right. My brother and I abandoned the Order when it was taken over by Boswell. Now he owns the Order, and our old leader, Captain Pike, refuses to make a stand against him. He's allowed the Order to be taken over."

Jasmine knew they were pressed for time. "What did Boswell want the Order to do?"

Jericho interrupted again, "He wants us to join his war. Boswell has a man named Dr. Maximus working for him. He's moving them right along. We need to put an end to Boswell and the Order before they take out everyone in the country."

Jasmine understood what they were doing there. Stop the war before it begins. "Where are we right now?"

Jericho told her, "This is the Bronx. The year is 2050."

"That gives us just enough time to stop this. What has Boswell already accomplished?" Jasmine needed to know where to start.

Jericho rudely answered, "He's working on the Kingdom. We'll all be dead by the time you get a move on."

Kim trusted in God. "This is a good sign. Tell us everything you know so we can stop this."

Gabriel continued walking with them, explaining, "The members of the Order that left Captain Pike have also brought along a lot of soldiers. Their families followed them. Right now, we're hiding because Pike and his men are trying to hunt us. It'll only be a matter of time before we're shot on sight. Several of our people were just slaughtered recently."

Jericho added, "The last of the survivors in the Deserters are at this location. If we just stay alive long enough to follow through with our plans, we'll stand a chance at defeating Boswell."

Jasmine asked, "What plan do you have?"

Gabriel stopped when they reached another large room where most of the deserters were resting, eating scraps, and praying for a miracle. Gabriel faced the people with an announcement, "These are friends of ours. They've come to help us. God has kept His promise to deliver us all. We'll make it through this. Keep praying."

Jericho sat down. "We've gotten lucky they haven't found us here."

Gabriel offered, "I'll send some men up to get the others in your group. We don't want them to be seen by the Order."

Jericho rose to his feet. "Hell, I'll go get them." He sprinted for the exit with some men.

Jasmine strolled around the room studying the behavior of their men. She approached a picture on the wall. The frame was partially covered with spiders' webs and dust. She wiped most of it away with a single stroke of her hand, exposing a clear view of the man in the photograph. An older gentleman sitting in the Oval Office with blonde hair combed over and a fierce stare in his eyes. Jasmine took a step back. "I've read about him. He was a good leader."

Gabriel agreed, "Yes. Sometimes when I feel overwhelmed about Boswell and the Order, I think of him. They tried several assassination attempts on his life and failed. God had plans for him. He has plans for you, too. When the going gets tough, always remember to take that man's advice and fight."

Kim poured some fresh water into jugs and cups around the room for the soldiers and civilians. Gabriel stood with a shocked expression on his face. "So, this is Divinity?!"

Jasmine smiled. "You've heard of her?"

"Yes. We were told about her before." Gabriel watched Kim pour Divinity in every cup and bowl they had available.

Redford continued petting Stooge. "We have a lot to talk about."

Jasmine was glad to see they were so helpful. She changed the subject. "So how do you and the Deserters plan to fight the Order and Boswell? How many of you can actually fight?"

"Jericho and I are the only real soldiers. The others refuse to leave their families behind, and we don't blame them. That's why we're here in the first place. We need to keep the families safe. Jericho and I were some of Captain Pike's best men."

Jasmine commended them for their courage. "That's very brave of you. Do you know where the Kingdom is located to destroy it?"

"The Kingdom isn't the problem right now. We need to deal with the Compound."

Kim joined the conversation, "What's the Compound?"

Gabriel told them, "That's the area they're working on right now. It's in the heart of the Bronx. The Order is also there. It's a large building beside it. If we succeed with taking out the Compound, the Kingdom won't be a problem for us."

Jericho returned with Sinclair. "The other member of your team is outside with some of our men. He won't be able to fit down here."

Jasmine smiled at Sinclair. "Nice of you to join us. You're just in time to hear what we need to do to take out Boswell."

Sinclair sat down with his weapon. "I'm all ears. I'm surprised nobody's killed him yet."

Gabriel grinned. "He's a slippery character."

Jericho paced the room with a scowl on his face. "Captain Pike is just as guilty as Boswell if you ask me!"

Jasmine wanted to keep them on track. "So, what have you come up with so far?"

Gabriel paused a moment before giving them the bad news. "The truth is we don't really know where to go from here. We just know that the Compound needs to be destroyed first. Take that out because that's where all the work and manpower is. Everything will fall apart once you take that out. We just haven't come up with a real plan yet."

Redford sighed, "You've got to be kidding me. You've literally been waiting for us to handle this? That's great."

Jasmine looked on the bright side. "We wouldn't be here if there wasn't a way to handle this. If the Compound needs to be destroyed, it'll be done."

Kim agreed, "We can do this with no problem. We've had Boswell on the run before."

Jericho crossed his arms. "Well, what are you waiting for?"

Kim grabbed hold of her vial. "We've located the Deserters. Where do we go from here?"

Divinity began to shimmer in the vial. "He's coming."

Everyone stood in awe and marveled as they witnessed Divinity shimmer and speak. Kim took a deep breath before asking with concern, "Who's coming?"

A man sprinted into the room saying, "I was told we had company!"

Every member of the Chronicles stared at the man when they realized it was Wrench. They rushed over to him, taking turns greeting and embracing him with affection. They knew Wrench hadn't met them yet because they went back in time, but it was still a delight having him standing there in front of them. Redford was happy to see him. "Nice to see you made it."

Wrench ignored her comment, "I'm assuming you're the ones God's sent us to stop this war."

Redford was thrilled to have their old friend back. "That's right."

Kim asked Wrench, "Did you have a name for the dog?"

Wrench shrugged his shoulders. "Not really."

Kim knelt over to pet him. "You called him Stooge in the future." She chuckled at how strange it sounded saying that to him.

Wrench complimented the brothers on their good work, "It looks like you guys can handle it from here. Let me know if you need me for anything." Wrench exited the room, and Stooge followed behind.

Gabriel announced, "When you and your team are ready, Crescendo, we can show you around and get a plan in order. The sooner we take out that property, the better." Jasmine couldn't agree more. The entire situation was risky and complicated, but they were no strangers to dangerous missions. Jasmine was just grateful to have located the Deserters as soon as they did.

June 14th.

Pike sat across the table from Stamina and Kibosh. The Strikers kept their eyes glued on him to the point he was beginning to feel uncomfortable. They agreed to the meeting but weren't expecting it to be very long. They knew it involved Boswell, so the payment would be worth it, but they felt the same about Boswell as everyone else.

Pike glanced at Cross and Hendrix sitting next to each other a few chairs away. He let out a long sigh, knowing that he wouldn't get anything accomplished if Hendrix took over the meeting. He remained focused. "It's been a long time. How have you been?"

Kibosh scowled at him. "How do you think?"

Pike didn't want to argue with them right off the bat. "Relax, Kibosh." He asked Stamina, "Are you keeping Kibosh in line? I know how easy it is for her to lose her temper. I've heard stories."

Kibosh was proud of her reputation: "They're all true."

Cross placed her assault rifle on the chair next to her. "Answer a question for me."

He nodded. "Of course. I will if I can."

She brushed her hair behind her shoulders. "Why would a man like Boswell want us working for him? Furthermore, how could you be foolish enough to expect us to take the job?"

Pike replied, "Cross, I'm not here as an enemy but as a friend."

Cross raised her eyebrows before turning to Hendrix. "Did you hear that? Pike means us no harm. I'm not sure if I'm convinced."

Hendrix felt differently about him: "I have nothing against him." She wanted to give him a chance: "You've asked if you could meet with us, and we accepted. What you don't realize is that we don't have a permanent residence. How much of anything will belong to us if we agree to work for a monster like Boswell? He'll take us for everything we have."

Pike calmly replied, "Have some faith." He leaned back in his chair and scanned the surroundings of an old, worn room falling apart. The establishment was a condemned two-story hotel that had been half burnt during a fire years prior. Only a couple of rooms in there were left standing, and the main lobby was more like a meeting area. It worked as shelter during travel. Pike stated the obvious: "You could do much better. I've seen your skills in action. Working for Boswell will give you a chance to get away from here."

Kibosh reminded Hendrix, "Boswell is known for killing his own men after they've served their purpose. I don't feel comfortable working for someone like that."

Hendrix ignored her and asked Pike, "If we agree to join you, what's the payment going to be?"

Pike was honest: "I can't guarantee you'll get anything from Boswell, but I can promise you anything you discover along the way is up for grabs. You might get lucky with some random jobs while you're working for us. He's allowed that. Take advantage of it."

Cross grinned. "So, I guess you didn't hear the news."

"Will you fill me in?" Pike didn't need any surprises.

She answered, "We're not bounty hunters anymore."

Hendrix was looking forward to telling him, "Being a mercenary is guaranteed work and good money. As you know, we're all soldiers."

Pike was caught off guard. "Why did you give it up?"

Stamina offered, "There's a reason why we quit. Want to hear about it?"

Pike nodded. "I'd like to know."

Hendrix interrupted, making it a very short story: "The bounties were being stolen from us after we met you years ago. We found out that the men worked for Boswell. They would use our bounties for extra jobs on the side. We can hold our own, but taking on the entire Order would be suicide. The way we see it is Boswell owes us already. His men have been ripping us off for a long time. One way or another we're getting payment from that man. Maybe we can take his ship once it's finished."

Pike understood why they felt the way they did. "I understand. I'm hoping you can get past this, and perhaps we can work something out. There's got to be a way we can help each other. I'm willing to try if you are."

Cross chimed in, "You might want to keep his men away from us if we accept."

Pike admitted, "It's wrong what his men did. I can't change that, but I can promise you this trip will be worth it. You'll be on board the

Kingdom with us."

Cross shook her head, denying it. "They'll never get that thing built."

Pike replied, "Dr. Maximus is working on it. It'll be complete and fueled very soon."

Hendrix didn't understand, "What are Boswell's plans?"

Pike lowered his head before answering, "You've been given a golden ticket. Take it or leave it. Trust me, you'll wish you were on board the Kingdom."

Hendrix waved her index finger at Pike with disappointment. "You've sold your soul to be alongside Boswell. You'll regret that sooner rather than later. Nobody gets a seat at his table without risking something. What did you give up for all this? I thought you were better than this."

Kibosh added, "You have yourself a master now."

Stamina joined in, "You're moving up in the world, Pike."

They watched Pike stand up and head for the door. Hendrix asked, "What would it take for you to turn your back on him?"

Pike placed his hands on his hips and slowly faced them. "Are you insane?"

Stamina added, "You have the Order to help you do it."

Pike approached the table. "Even if my men were up for the task, there's no way we could take out Boswell. All he needs to do is press the panic button, and we'll have the entire Revival family on our ass."

Hendrix was surprised. "It sounds like you're scared of them."

He corrected her, "I'm terrified!"

Hendrix knew he meant well with the meeting. "You've extended your hand to us, and I thank you for that. I think Cross, Kibosh, and Stamina are wrong about you. I always knew there was another side to you, Pike. I just don't see any real promise in joining a man like Boswell."

Pike tried convincing them, "There will always be another Boswell. When he's dead and gone, somebody else will replace him."

Hendrix rose to her feet and strolled around the table. "You're right, but there are also people that stand against monsters like Boswell."

Pike had realized Hendrix and the others had become more human than when he first met them. "You'll die if you don't join us, and you'll die if you try killing Boswell. I can't help you after I leave here today. This is a once-in-a-lifetime opportunity." He locked eyes with Hendrix with all seriousness. "Please don't pass on this chance."

Hendrix turned to her team, asking, "How do you girls feel about joining a monster on board the Kingdom?"

Kibosh agreed, "Sounds like we'd be foolish not to take the chance."

Stamina broke down, "To hell with it. We might as well join them. What else do we have going for us?"

Cross sighed, "Why can't we just kill Boswell now?" She knew that was a stupid question. "Yeah, whatever. Let's do this. I'm in."

Pike was pleased. "I can send for you when Boswell is ready."

Stamina asked curiously, "Who else will be on board the Kingdom?"

Pike didn't tell them much: "A woman named Offspring will be tagging along with us. Boswell also has a friend from the Revival that will be nearby. His name is Brawler. I believe he's being stationed in California, though."

Cross wasn't impressed. "That's it? The rest are your soldiers from the Order?"

Hendrix laid down the law: "Boswell might think he's running the show, but he better stay on my good side. I'll obey orders for only so long before I make a stand."

Pike was aware of their behavior. "You might get lucky. Boswell isn't a mutant. He just might get killed before any of this ever takes off. Once we're on board the Kingdom, be professional."

Cross joined in, "So I guess we'll stick around here and wait for you to call for us? We'll be waiting. In the meantime, there have been deserters spotted in the area, Pike. We know Boswell's been trying to kill them off."

Pike felt guilty. "I've been ordered to kill them and their families." He reached up to rub his face. "It goes along with the job. I'm the one that answers for it."

Hendrix changed the subject. "That's it then. Let us know when you're ready."

Pike watched them gawk at him. He wasn't sure if he was making a mistake or not. He knew they were useful but didn't want to push his luck. Pike wasn't the only one taking a chance. Hendrix and her crew would be in the same position. Pike headed for the door to make his exit. "I'll be in touch."

Hendrix chuckled at him, "Why in such a hurry to leave?! Do we make you uncomfortable?!"

Pike turned to her but remained at the threshold of the door. "Boswell's kept me busy. I have a lot of work to do."

Hendrix approached him. She reached out to place her hands across his chest. "You poor man. When will you ever have time for yourself?"

Pike pushed her hands away. "I don't have time for this." He glared at Hendrix. "Is there anything else on your mind before I leave?"

Hendrix took a few steps back after realizing he wasn't weak enough to seduce. "Big strong man has a busy job to get back to." She turned to join the others at the table in the lobby. Hendrix sat down. "Stay awhile and have a drink with us, Pike."

He turned for the door again. "I'm not interested."

Hendrix watched him escape her web. "See you soon, Pike!" She let out a heavy sigh. "How do you feel about this? Does anyone want to kick-start a meeting?"

Kibosh approached the front window and watched Pike's vehicle disappear in the distance. "I could care less. We still need to eat and get better equipment. That's not free, and Boswell will pay well, even if he is a monster."

Hendrix snapped her fingers at Kibosh, "So, you're in favor of Pike!" She turned to Stamina, "You're next."

Stamina was always sporting a neutral attitude: "Whatever needs to get done, I'm in." She quickly added, "For all we know, this could lead us somewhere."

Kibosh turned to the group. "I agree. If we can't strike it rich, at least give us a change of scenery. And I never thought I'd say this, but get me out of New York before it starts snowing."

Hendrix watched Cross sit there staring off into outer space, deep in thought. She snapped her fingers in her face. "What's the verdict? Are you in favor of Pike or not?"

Cross turned to them. "Let's do it. Maybe this time we won't come back to this hellhole."

Kibosh stood with her arms crossed. "Wishful thinking. It'll take a miracle to get out of here."

Hendrix headed for the stairs. "We'll be better off leaving. I'm thinking Pike will be back in a day or two. I want to be ready for him when he arrives. Let's not keep Boswell waiting."

THE DESERTERS

6:43 P.M.

The view was perfect. Jasmine and Kim stood at the back room staring out the window with Gabriel and Jericho. They had brought the two of them there to see for themselves what the Compound looked like. The heart of the Bronx had been completely torn apart and rebuilt to serve Boswell and his upcoming war. Not far from their location was where the Kingdom was also being worked on by Dr. Maximus. Jasmine and Kim witnessed and lived Boswell's war firsthand. They were there to put an end to it.

Jericho stepped back to lean against the wall after having a final look at the Compound. Everyone walked away from the window after taking a long look. Jasmine kick-started the conversation. "So, what's the plan? What would be the best way to destroy the Compound without endangering any innocent lives?"

Jericho annoyingly asked, "You've got to be kidding me! You don't know of any way to destroy it? I thought you were sent here with answers!"

Jasmine assured them, "We'll take care of it. Just focus on keeping the civilians safe."

Gabriel maintained the peace. He gave the Chronicles the respect they deserved: "You have the answers for us. I have faith you can do this."

Kim clutched the vial of water. "Divinity said she will guide us."

Jericho grew frustrated by the minute. They had been fighting off the enemy and hiding in fear for far too long. "We're running out of time here. Boswell has his men working around the clock. He'll be airborne by the time we make a move."

Gabriel informed the Chronicles, "There's nothing anyone can do to stop Boswell. You're our only chance. The military and the government won't step forward. They've allowed him to take over. The state of New York is under the mind control of the Revival family."

Kim held onto her vial until it began to shimmer. Divinity spoke, "Tomorrow. Be ready."

Gabriel and Jericho stood there in awe after witnessing the power of Divinity once again. Jasmine was relieved. "Tell us what to do. Give us the answer we need."

Divinity shimmered while speaking, "Take me to the Order. I will tell you when."

Jericho thought about how risky it was going to be. "Captain Pike and his men will find us!"

Jasmine was shocked to hear his name, "Captain Pike?!"

Gabriel nodded. "Yeah, we figured you'd know him."

Kim had to keep in mind they were in another time. "We know what will happen if we don't stop Boswell. We've lived it."

Jericho warned them, "Captain Pike has thousands of soldiers. They will kill you if you're caught."

Divinity interrupted them, "Trust in God."

Jasmine tried figuring out a plan. "Where does Boswell spend his time? Not just at the Order."

Gabriel told her, "He has a lot of property. He does have a home here in the Bronx. Captain Pike also has a place here."

Jasmine told them, "Get the rest of the deserters and lead them out of town. I can leave some of my men with you to make sure you all get out safely."

Gabriel asked, "And what will you do?"

Jasmine pointed to Kim. "Until Divinity tells us it's time, we need to remain in hiding."

Jericho crossed his arms. "I'm ok with that plan."

Gabriel wanted to help. "I can come with you."

"Thank you, but we need you and your brother to lead the others out of the Bronx. After the Compound is destroyed, Boswell and his men will be hunting us all."

Jericho was trying to look at it in a good way: "At least their work will be blown to hell. They'll still have their soldiers. How will we stop them or even outrun them?"

Jasmine answered, "I'm not sure. We'll cross that bridge when we get to it."

Kim wanted to make sure they were prepared. "We should get back and inform the others."

Gabriel was still concerned for their safety. "Just the two of you are going to the Compound?"

Jasmine told them, "No, we'll bring Cinder with us. Machine and Fedora will stay behind. When we leave, that's when you'll need to lead everyone out of the Bronx. No matter what happens, just keep moving. We'll meet with you when we're through."

Jericho asked, "How will you find us?"

Jasmine replied, "That's not what you should be worried about right now." She watched Gabriel and Jericho lead the way back to the others to warn them.

CHAPTER NINE

THE TOWER

Manhattan, New York.

Boswell sat at his desk observing the recently hired help. The woman named Trinity appeared to be in her early forties and wore a green and black camouflage uniform. She was unarmed at the moment but was said to have been an excellent marksman with any weapon. She stared with her green eyes across the desk at Boswell, waiting for him to speak. The silence in the room was beginning to annoy her.

The second hired gun wore black and purple combat gear with a black mask over his face. He was unwilling to show his true appearance. His name was Dallas. He appeared to be very professional but turned out to be more of an arrogant risk taker but still managed to get the job done. Dallas slowly stood up and began strolling around the room, curiously studying his surroundings. "I was wondering when the Revival would stick me with you, Boswell."

Trinity was already growing tiresome of Dallas. "I've never met the Revival. If they've teamed you up with Boswell, I'm sure there's good reason for it."

Boswell leaned forward in his chair, pointing across the desk.

"I assure you working for me will have its privileges as well as its punishments. Make sure you remain on the greener side of life."

Trinity noted what he said and moved on. "Your name travels. Are you really a member of the Revival?"

"No, not anymore. My parents were for many years."

Trinity replied, "I've heard about your parents. They helped put the Revival on the map. Why didn't you follow in their footsteps?"

Boswell gave his retort, "Who's to say I haven't?"

Dallas smirked behind his mask. "What makes you think you're up to the challenge?"

Boswell wasn't amused. "You've got a pair. I would stop while I'm ahead if I were you."

Dallas put his hands out peacefully while sarcastically replying, "Whatever you say, boss."

"Don't get too comfortable with me, son." Boswell wasn't in the mood.

Dallas reminded him, "Pike has gone out of his way to make sure we were here."

Boswell repaid the favor: "Pike works for me. I will always have the last say in everything. Get used to it."

Trinity asked Boswell, "Do you mind me asking why you need the extra help? What makes you think you need more help anyway? The Order is run by Captain Pike. Can't he give you more men?"

Boswell answered her reasonable question, "For this particular help I need more qualified assistance." He turned to Dallas, asking, "May I ask you why you took this job?"

Dallas nodded. "I thought I'd see how far you've come along since the Revival allowed you to stay with them. I've worked for them before in the past but never had the opportunity to get the full experience I was hoping for until now. I wanted to see how much of your parents is inside your work."

He replied, "I hate to disappoint you, but Dr. Maximus is doing most of the work for me alongside my engineers. I'm on a clock. I've never enjoyed wasting time, Dallas. That's one thing you'll learn quickly about me."

Dallas stopped and turned to him. "We have plenty of time to get to know each other. I heard you brought Poison and Brawler in on this."

He shot back, "Don't speak of things that aren't any of your concern. They're assigned to their locations, and you'll have no involvement with them."

Dallas smirked, "Whatever you say, boss."

Boswell wanted to see what they knew. "How much has Pike told you?"

"I heard about the Kingdom through the grapevine," Dallas replied proudly. "When you're working on something that big, it's impossible to keep it quiet."

Boswell knew what kind of man he was dealing with. "You hear a lot, don't you?"

"It's hard not to hear about a man that's trying to start his own personal war. You and the Order have cleared out the Bronx for a reason. I'm amazed the Revival family is even letting you do it. Everybody's been relocated to different cities for safety. I heard the Revival didn't care just as long as nobody from the state of New York was involved or endangered."

Boswell watched Dallas stand with a satisfied expression on his face. "You're well informed. Do you plan on continuing your services for the family once you're finished with me?"

Dallas shrugged his shoulders. "I haven't thought that far ahead."

Trinity joined in, "Where is Captain Pike? I thought he was going to be here."

Boswell nodded to her. "He will be here soon, my dear." He stood up and walked around to the front of his desk. "I have a surprise to show you once Pike's arrived."

Trinity stated, "Hopefully the surprise isn't far. I've traveled a long way to be here."

"Believe me, it'll be worth your time."

Dallas wanted to know more about his plans. "So, what's going on with the Kingdom?"

"What do you mean? Boswell was already annoyed with him and couldn't help but wonder why the Revival family would have used his services in the past. They were either foolish, or he was surprisingly very professional when the time came."

"I hear it's a special place for only a few chosen people. It's nice to see we fall in that special upper crust of society. Only certain people matter to you wealthy individuals."

Boswell glanced over at Trinity and saw that she was still trying to catch up in the conversation. Was it because she didn't care or because she's heard these stories before? Boswell was making a name for himself regardless if he wanted to or not. Trinity caught Boswell's stare, and she asked, "Pike was saying there's no telling how long the job will be. Is that true?"

Boswell locked eyes with her. "That's right. Are you squeamish about this kind of work?"

"That depends on what kind of work we're really doing for you." She hinted to him that there was more going on here. She wasn't a fool.

"Are the two of you here for the job or to get on board the Kingdom because you know what will happen if you're not?"

Dallas shot back, "Don't worry about it. It won't affect our work. I don't know anything about Trinity, but she appears to be as much of a professional as I am."

Boswell told them, "I need people I can rely on. You seem to fit the bill. Don't forget why you're with us. Just stay with Pike, and he'll show you what's expected. Offspring is more hired help. She'll also be shadowing Pike."

Dallas was talking too much: "The aircraft will hold a lot of passengers, right?"

Boswell turned to give him the look of death. "That doesn't concern you."

Trinity offered her services while they waited to board the Kingdom. "I've heard you're after the Deserters. Would you like help clearing them out while we wait?"

Boswell was shocked at how well informed they were. "You know about them?"

She answered, "I know Captain Pike and the Order had some recent trouble with some runaways. We figured you needed our help taking them out. When we got here Dallas and I thought perhaps you would need us for the cockroach problem too. That's what I was expecting."

Boswell told them, "Pike is a good man, but he lacks in certain ways."

Dallas asked, "Which way?"

Boswell answered, "To follow orders." He sat back down at his desk. "Pike has a problem with killing families. I'm hoping the two of you will be able to pick up his slack."

Dallas was cold-hearted: "I'll kill whoever you want."

Boswell grinned. "Perhaps I misjudged you, Dallas."

"I'm just trying to break the ice, boss." Dallas gave him a cocky grin. "I'm here to follow orders, not have a conscience."

The office door opened. Boswell stood up, pointing to the table for the guests to have a seat. "Captain Pike, have a seat." He nodded to Offspring. "Thank you for coming, Offspring. Join us!"

Pike apologized, "Sorry we're late."

Offspring was hesitant at first with the new help. She pulled out a chair but remained standing. She studied the hired help. "We got held up."

Boswell made an excuse for them: "Pike's a busy man. I'm sure there's good reason for it. You're both here now. That's all that matters."

Pike sat down. "It won't happen again."

Dallas decided to have some fun with Offspring. "No wonder you guys hired us. If this is the help you've got, then you're in trouble."

Trinity watched a fierce stare in her eyes stare him down. "I don't think so, Dallas. This one seems to be the real deal."

Dallas disagreed, "She'll need to prove herself."

Boswell moved right along before things escalated. "Offspring is very professional. I need her. In time all of you will understand why." He pointed to Offspring, introducing them officially. "This is Trinity and Dallas. You can thank Pike for hiring them."

Pike turned to Offspring, ordering her, "Have a seat."

She sat down next to Pike. "Let's get on with it."

Boswell agreed, "Yes, shall we?"

Pike kickstarted the meeting. "My men displayed the dead deserters out where they can be seen. I doubt we'll have any trouble out of them."

Boswell sighed, "You're a fool if you believe this is as far as they'll go."

Dallas asked, "How did this happen in the first place?"

Pike explained himself, "Deserters are just runaways from the Order. I know you know this, Dallas. Why should I explain it to you?"

Dallas placed his hands in the air. "Guilty as charged. I just wanted to see if any parts of the story were left out."

Boswell stood up while announcing, "Dr. Maximus is tucked away finishing the Kingdom. It's nearly complete. He's left us a gift in the next room. I'd like all of you to see it together."

Pike was clueless as to what was going on. "Didn't you have Dr. Maximus work on something for you recently?"

"He's finished it," Boswell replied.

Dallas was impressed with the stories he heard of Maximus. "The man seems to know what he's doing. Didn't Dr. Maximus work for the Revival too?"

Boswell wanted to move on. "He's a brilliant man. Leave it at that." He walked across the room, saying, "You've been the lucky chosen one, Offspring."

She asked curiously, "What do you mean?"

"Dr. Maximus has created an ultimate soldier at my request. I didn't have a doubt in my mind that he could do it. Never mind the details of how he made this possible. That story is for another time. The important thing is that Offspring will possess its power for now. Think of this opportunity as controlling your own personal invisible man. Or an entity, perhaps."

Offspring stood up unsure of what to expect. "What is it Maximus created this time?"

Trinity was getting anxious. "Show us what it is!"

Boswell stepped out into the center of the room. "I'm hoping we can all work together on this. Very soon this will be a new world. I want all of you to be part of it."

Pike stood up and led the way to the office door. Everyone followed him into the hallway. "This should be interesting."

Boswell took the lead and opened two double doors to a room across the hall. They all entered and saw that it was a small lab inside. There were several different workstations, tools, and materials organized and labeled throughout the room. Boswell approached a table in the back and stepped aside while pointing to a whistle. "There it is. The ultimate soldier."

Dallas stared at the whistle. "Something's missing."

Boswell corrected him, "Not exactly."

Trinity stepped forward to get a look. "Tell us what we're looking at here."

Pike stood there gawking at it in awe. "Maximus pulled it off?"

Boswell smiled. "I told you he could do it. He's created Umbra, an invisible soldier, or, like I said, an entity. The power of the collected abilities from several mutants has been harnessed from the subjects and infused into the ultimate experiment, creating a warrior that can be controlled only by this whistle. Anyone that carries this with them possesses its power. The rest you'll learn along the way. This is why Dr. Maximus has worked with us over the years."

Offspring shook her head repeatedly, "Why me?"

Boswell reached over, grabbing the whistle that was attached to a necklace, and placed it around her neck. "Because I trust you."

Pike wanted to make sure they were on schedule. "Where is Dr. Maximus?"

Boswell straightened his tie, confident of his plans falling into place. "He's where he belongs. He won't budge until the job is complete, unless he wants his granddaughter to get a bullet in her."

Offspring tucked the whistle inside her uniform. "Will we be the first to board the Kingdom?"

Boswell answered with a look of satisfaction, "Yes, of course. It is my aircraft."

Trinity interrupts, "Now that we've seen the dog and pony show, I'd like to get to work if you don't mind."

Boswell grinned, "You're an ambitious woman. I'll give you that." He turned to Pike, telling him, "Take Dallas and Trinity downstairs and see that they're looked after until we need their services."

Offspring asked, "And what about me?"

Boswell answered, "You stay with me. I'm going to have some tests run on you in the lab. Not to worry, darling," he explained himself as Pike and the others left the room. "I'm going to make sure you and your new friend Umbra are very comfortable with each other. This is a minor experiment Maximus had run by me earlier today. I've chosen you to be part of history. You'll be out of here in no time." Offspring didn't argue with him. She was intrigued.

CHAPTER TEN

THE COMPOUND

June 15th.

It seems like only yesterday when we stood against Boswell. I never expected to make it this far. It feels so surreal. With our experiences in Mystic Cloud and now being sent out on missions from God, it's overwhelming and yet so fulfilling. There's still much I'm not sure about, but I know we're exactly where we're meant to be.

After going through the portal, I never expected to show up back in New York. Locating the Deserters has helped us lay low while we waited for Divinity to guide us through our mission. As I write this passage, I feel at ease knowing that the Deserters are being led to safety by Fedora and Machine. After destroying the Compound, we will regroup with our team to follow through with the rest of our mission. God be with us all. – Crescendo

Jasmine was resting alongside the stacks of material they were using for the Compound. She scanned the area while keeping down low. Redford and Kim were kneeling next to her, glaring out past the construction site, and could see the entrance to the Order. Redford observed only a few soldiers making their rounds. "This might be easier than I thought."

Kim was shocked to see that the men were leaving. "I was expecting more?"

Jasmine remained focused. "I don't care what it looks like. Keep your eyes open out here. I don't want to get caught off guard."

Redford sighed, "Soon we'll be up against Pike again. It's a different time, so he hasn't met us yet. He's as bad as Boswell right now. Keep that in mind if he corners you."

Kim made a note of it: "There you go again, Cinder. Always digging up the past."

Redford smirked, "Whatever, just remember to keep Divinity ready for us."

Jasmine remained low to the ground as she watched a bigger group of soldiers stopping outside the entrance of the Order. They began talking with each other just before turning to make their rounds through the property. Jasmine sighed heavily. "That's not good."

Redford glared down and saw the soldiers. "We can take them easily."

Kim needed to ask a serious question: "Are we aiming to kill or just destroy the compound?"

Jasmine answered, "Try to avoid killing the soldiers if you can. We're not here for that."

Redford knew Jasmine was going to spare their lives. "They're trying to kill us, Crescendo."

"I realize that, Cinder." Jasmine knew she would give her an issue about it.

Divinity suddenly spoke, "She's right, Crescendo."

Jasmine turned to stare at Redford. She watched as a grin came over her. "Are you happy now, Cinder?" Divinity says, "Kill the soldiers."

She shook it off. "Never mind that; let's just get this done."

Jasmine nodded. "Just keep low. There's only about ten guards, but they can still be a problem."

They rushed down a small hill through the construction area and froze simultaneously after being caught by two of the guards as they walked around the corner. One of them shouted into his earpiece, "Intruders!" The soldiers scattered across the property.

The two guards raised their assault rifles. Remedy didn't have time to think and pulled her pistol faster than them, shooting them several times at close range. She froze out of shock, realizing what she had done. Jasmine pulled Kim for cover while the rest of the soldiers opened fire on them. Jasmine snapped her out of the daze. "You've done this before, Remedy! We know you didn't mean it! I need you to focus!"

Redford rushed out towards the enemy. "I'll keep them busy!"

Jasmine kept low, running through a pathway that wrapped around the Compound. They continued on down another short hill, sliding closer to the foundation of the property. Jasmine shouted to Kim as they got closer to the building, "Get Divinity! We need her!"

In the distance one of the soldiers yelled out, "Do you see them?! Spread out!"

A soldier replied while pointing towards the Chronicles, "There's two down here! We can take them!"

Another guard yelled out, "Flush them out!" He turned to wave at one of his men. "Send for backup!"

Jasmine formed a handful of orbs in her hand. "Like hell you will!" She ran out in the open, throwing them to the far side of the Compound. The explosion knocked over a large crane, taking out two of the soldiers.

Jasmine rushed for cover again, yelling, "Cinder! Don't fall asleep on us!"

Redford jumped over one of the hummers in front of the property, racing over to Kim. Three-armed soldiers rush around the corner, spotting her. Redford yelled, "Remedy, look out!" She abruptly stopped and threw up her hands, forming a wall of fire separating them from the bad guys. The heat of the flames forces the soldiers to pull back.

Kim stood aside watching Redford form a wall of fire across the property, keeping them all at bay. She pointed to the Compound, "Keep them busy!" Kim returned to the foundation of the structure.

Jasmine formed several more orbs in her hands and bounced them across the field, keeping the enemy away. She knelt close to the ground, waving Kim to the property. "Come on! Let's get this over with! What are you waiting for?!"

A soldier could be heard shouting out across the way, "There's only three of them!"

The soldiers frantically searched for a way past the wall of fire. Another soldier yelled back, "There's no way through! Get the troops here!"

Kim reached the foundation and stopped to catch her breath. "Work through me, Divinity."

Divinity replied, "Place your hands across the foundation."

Kim closed her eyes, reaching out to touch the structure of the Compound. After feeling the release of Divinity, she spread across the building, covering it with shimmering light blue water. Kim opened her eyes and stood in awe at the sight of it as the building was being covered with the power of Divinity. She took a step back, shaking her head. "Cinder, I think we need to get out of here!" The sounds of cracking and breaking echoed across the property.

Redford continued shooting her fire towards the enemy. "What's wrong?!"

Kim shouted and pointed to the compound, "Run! The building's about to collapse!"

Jasmine raced out from across the field, meeting the others towards the front. "Let's move out! Get going!" Jasmine could hear strange noises as if it were about to fall apart all at once. The water around the building ate away at the foundation, weakening it by the second.

Redford turned to take cover. "We can't outrun this! Keep your heads down!"

Jasmine met up with the others. They all tried running back up the hill to the top but couldn't. Jasmine shouted, "It's too steep!" The ground was crumbling beneath their feet in that area.

Kim shouted out, "Divinity, help us!" Suddenly their bodies were surrounded by the shimmering light blue water as it began levitating them safely from the construction area and placed them back at the top of the hill. The water had disappeared, leaving the three of them standing in a row to watch as the Compound came tumbling down in multiple sections, destroying everything Boswell had been working on throughout the property.

Redford started laughing and clapped her hands at the sight of it. "Take that, Boswell!"

Jasmine let out a sigh of relief. "We just stopped the Kingdom, ladies. Again." She wiped sweat from her forehead, announcing, "Somewhere underneath all that rubble is Boswell's aircraft."

Kim was speechless for a moment. She placed her right hand across her heart. "Thank you, Lord." She laughed it off now that she knew that part of the mission was complete. "We didn't know how we were going to do this at first, remember! God's definitely a way maker!"

After taking in the sight of a mission accomplished, Redford and Kim turned to their leader, awaiting their next orders. Redford grinned. "What's next, Crescendo?"

Kim was exhausted but needed to move on. "Fedora and Machine probably have a safe place for the Deserters by now." She took a moment to catch her breath. "Boswell will come for us."

Jasmine smirked. She turned to head for the Harpoon with them. "It wouldn't be the first time." She hopped into the driver seat, suggesting, "Perhaps we should hunt him for a change."

THE TOWER

Manhattan, New York.

After the tests had been completed and Boswell was finished with Offspring, he had sent for her yet again to have a word in private. Boswell never relied on only one person that worked for him; he relied on many to pull together, making his life easier. If he felt there was a way to get what he needed, he would go as far as putting his own crew against each other. Boswell needed someone to trust with Umbra. He couldn't use Pike because he was the captain of the guards.

Offspring stood outside on the balcony of the Tower looking out across the property. She watched Boswell approach her with a bottle of champagne and two glasses. He placed them on a table and began pouring until the glasses were full. "How are you feeling?"

Offspring took a glass from him, "I'm still alive. You were right; the procedure didn't take long. I'm not one hundred percent sure what happened, but I'm fine."

He was pleased. "Of course you are, my dear. Umbra is now part of you. We wanted to see if it were possible to combine human life with the experiment. As you can see, it's safe. If our studies are correct, whenever you use the whistle when you're in danger, Umbra will now have a direct connection to who to save during times of trouble. You're joined together as one now."

She would need to get used to the idea. "It's surreal to think of it that way." She set her champagne down.

Boswell was insulted. "You refuse to drink with me?"

"I need to take off my mask to do so. I'd rather not."

Boswell smiled at her. He raised his glass out of respect. "To each their own." He took a sip and watched her stare out into the sky. "Do I make you nervous?" He made note of her behavior.

"Whatever gave you that idea?"

Boswell stepped closer to her. "You refuse to get close to me. You're always at a distance."

"I'm being professional. I would expect the same from you."

He smirked, "I don't know what it is I like about you!"

"Whatever it is, it got me on board the Kingdom," she replied.

He laughed before taking a sip of his champagne. "Now you're talking my language!"

Offspring kept him on that topic: "Do you have in mind where you'll be traveling first?"

"I have many things in mind." He watched her intently. "With your help and loyalty, I'll get what I want quickly."

Offspring wasn't surprised. "You're already thinking of more. Do you plan on leaving a part of this world for someone else to control?"

"I leave nothing for nobody." He leaned into her, asking, "Have you seen what happens when two leaders bump heads? There can never be two leaders. One will go his way, and the other will go another. Nothing will get accomplished." Boswell shook his head repeatedly. "That's not a life for me! Not me!"

She asked, "Then what?"

He took another sip of his champagne. "I'm not sure if I should say, although I planned on speaking to Pike about it sometime."

She turned to face him. "I thought you weren't on speaking terms."

"We are, my dear, but it's more like a lover's quarrel."

She kept at him just for fun, "You must really want those Deserters dead."

"I tend to get that way at times. Nobody quits on me. Nobody turns on me. I live by simple rules, a code of ethics if you will. They haven't failed me yet. The Deserters ran off on me and deserve death."

She nodded. "Uh huh, and has this code of ethics made you into the man you are now?"

"I like this side of you. I've never seen it before." He enjoyed speaking with her. He found her to be engaging. "Do I see many more conversations once we've boarded the Kingdom?"

"Perhaps that will happen."

Boswell wasn't expecting her to agree to it. "You're full of surprises. Why the sudden change of heart?"

She still kept her distance from him. "Perhaps we both want to know who we're working with."

Boswell was pleased to hear it. "Finally, common ground that levels the playing field. Life is always so much sweeter with honey, my dear."

"I agree."

He set his glass down and reached out to grab her hand. "Shall we dance?"

She snickered behind the mask, "There's no music."

He wanted to look into her soul to understand her: "We will make our own."

She allowed him to pull her aside for a moment. Boswell stood in the proper stance, gently holding her hand and upper waist. "I believe a waltz would be appropriate for the evening." He gave her a moment before leading into a slow waltz.

She was impressed, "I didn't know you could dance."

"The Revival family spared no expense at providing the lavish lifestyle that I grew accustomed to for many years. The upper crust of society is what I'm trying to keep alive. Only the very best shall continue to thrive in my world."

"I'm well aware of your plans, but what pleasure do you see in having the weak and poor become enslaved to the wealthy? Don't you find that to be monstrous?"

He chuckled at the humor of it. "Not at all! I'm doing them a favor!"

"And how is forcing enslavement a favor?"

Boswell answered, "By allowing the weak and the poor to live out their lives the way God intended it to be. Everyone has a part to play regardless of how hard it might be to accept that."

Offspring replied, "Correct me if I'm wrong, but I thought you were an atheist." She felt his hand squeeze hers with great pressure until she was uncomfortable. "You're hurting my hand, Winston."

He didn't enjoy being challenged. He stopped dancing abruptly and let her go. "Perhaps that's enough for one evening."

"Did I offend you?" She knew she did and didn't care.

He changed the subject: "You've been spending time with Pike."

She nodded. "He's a good man."

"He is indeed, and yet he has many flaws."

Offspring asked curiously, "What makes you doubt him?"

"Pike has an army, and I need them. They follow him because he's their leader. He has trouble following orders." Boswell was bothered with it. "Remember when I said there can't be two leaders? My professional relationship with Pike is suffering because of it."

"What has he not done to please you?"

He answered, "Certain orders, like killing women and children."

She yelled to him, "Maybe he doesn't want to be used that way!"

Boswell shouted back, "I'm using all of you! Don't you people get it?!"

She wasn't shocked that he was so blunt: "I knew I fell into your sights when we first met."

"And yet you still obey me. That's what I like about you."

Offspring calmed down. "It would be easier if you just told me what you're after."

He finished his drink. "Tell me what Pike's shared with you."

"He's shared a lot with me. What are you looking for? I hope you don't want me to stab him in the back. That's not my style." Offspring wouldn't budge.

"I wouldn't dream of you stabbing him in the back."

"Then what is it?" She waited for an answer.

Boswell came out with it: "Pike knows good help when he sees it, but lately his judgment stinks. He came to me recently with the idea of hiring the Strikers."

Offspring asked, "Do you have an issue with them?"

"Hendrix and her crew will be here soon. In the past they have been ripped off by my men. At one point their bounties were taken from them. They have reason to come here with a vendetta."

"Then why allow them on board?"

He shook the thought of it from his mind. "Perhaps heavy security would take care of the problem until I can figure out what to do with them, but things could be different if they wanted to bury the hatchet."

She doubted it, saying, "I don't think that'll happen."

"If they work with us, they could become very valuable to me. I just need someone to watch them for me. Keep an eye on them."

She saw no harm in it. "I'll be there to protect you. That's my job."

Boswell reached for her drink and took it for himself. "You're a brave woman and a liar. I don't mind when people keep things from me. In the end it'll only be hurting themselves. I truly hope you and I remain on the same page."

She didn't argue with him, "I won't be a problem for you."

Boswell was pleased. "I won't curse those for having their own agendas. Just don't let your ambitions interfere with mine. I'm sure you're wondering why I called you here this evening. I merely want to get to know my new bodyguard. I was also curious how you were feeling after the procedure. Everything seems to be in order."

She was flattered. "Thank you for caring. To make sure our

professional relationship is on par, I'll keep a close watch on the Strikers once they arrive. Whatever I hear, you'll hear."

Boswell finished the champagne. Captain Pike rushed out onto the balcony with a look of shock. "Sir, it's gone!"

Offspring tried calming him down, "Relax! What's going on?!"

Boswell tried making sense of it all. "What's gone?! What the hell are you talking about?!"

Pike yelled out, "There's a surveillance video! Come with me, now! You need to come with me, sir!"

Boswell threw the glass across the ground shattering it as he demanded, "Tell me what's going on, Pike!"

He gave him the terrible news: "The Order, the Compound, the Kingdom, and everything on the property have been destroyed!" The information took a moment to sink into Boswell's head. Pike calmed himself before continuing, "The kingdom is gone." Boswell turned as pale white as a ghost. Offspring was speechless. Pike regretfully suggested, "You need to see the video, sir. Come with me." He tried jolting Boswell out of his sudden shock, "Come with me, sir."

EPILOGUE

The longer Hendrix stayed at the hotel, the more useless she felt. She remembered bringing the Strikers to that location to hide out after a job. After a while it became routine to stop at the same place whenever they were in New York. At that point if anyone wanted to hunt them down, they wouldn't have a hard time finding them. Hendrix realized not many people were searching for them anymore. They were becoming irrelevant, which sent Hendrix into a midlife crisis. There was a time when the Strikers were the talk of the town.

Hendrix sat on the edge of her bed staring at her equipment. Everything was calm. She knew her team felt the same way. After a moment of silence, she stood up just as there was a knock at the door. "Yeah, who is it?"

Kibosh entered the room and leaned against the threshold, crossing her arms. "You need some fresh air. Maybe even a drink."

Hendrix didn't deny it. "You're probably right."

Kibosh jumped into it. "If you plan on accepting Pike's offer, we need to talk it over first."

"We have time to think it over."

Kibosh shut the door behind her. "Whatever we come up with, Stamina and Cross will agree. I hate Boswell just as much as everyone else, but we need to get on board with the Kingdom. Once we're there, we can plan whatever we want, but we're running out of time."

Hendrix grinned, "Nobody will miss him when he's dead. That' for sure."

"Do you remember what you've told us?" She waited to get Hendrix's attention before adding, "You said you'd take over the Kingdom if you ever had the opportunity. This could be it."

"I think you've lost your mind. He has an army."

Kibosh chuckled, "Has that stopped us before from doing anything? We can get the facts from Pike. He'll be able to give us the information we need. Boswell won't know what's going on if we're careful."

It didn't take much convincing for Hendrix: "Maybe we should meet Pike and get this plan set into motion."

Kibosh knew they were moving up in the world. "The others will back you up on this. We've suffered at the hands of Boswell and his men long enough. It's time we take what's rightfully ours."

Hendrix agreed, "Yes, but nothing happens to Pike. As for Boswell, we'll handle him later."

Kibosh grinned. "Are you getting sweet on Pike? That's not like you."

"He means us no harm. I'll return the favor," she answered.

Kibosh was moving right along. "There's no telling how long we'll be airborne. Probably awhile. We'll have plenty of time to figure out a plan. I'm sure it won't be difficult getting Pike on board."

Hendrix added, "If they catch wind of this before we're on board, we're screwed. So, keep it quiet for now. Once we're inside, Pike can handle security and keep them off our backs."

Kibosh agreed, "That'll give us plenty of time to bring Pike to our side. Perhaps we can keep him around. He might come in handy."

Hendrix ignored the comment, "I think our ship has finally come in, Kibosh. No more running down deadbeats for chump change and taking nickel and dime jobs." Hendrix suddenly sat quietly before saying, "That reminds me, do you know who I spotted the other day?"

Kibosh annoyingly replied, "Just tell me."

Hendrix locked eyes with her. "Our old nemesis Trinity."

Kibosh rose to her feet, making fists in anger. "Tell me you're not joking!"

"Calm down, Kibosh. We know Trinity hasn't worked around these parts in years. Maybe it's just a coincidence, or maybe she heard Pike was searching for help."

Kibosh exited the room with Hendrix. They walked down to the lobby and saw Stamina and Cross sitting at the table relaxing. Stamina kicked her feet across the table and leaned back in the chair. "What's wrong now, Kibosh? You seem pissed again."

Cross turned to greet her. "Have a drink with us. You'll feel better."

Kibosh ignored their comments. "Did Victoria tell you girls the news?"

Hendrix swiftly added, "Kibosh and I have been talking upstairs."

Stamina smirked, "That's never a good thing."

Kibosh replied, "Listen to what she has to say. You'll enjoy this."

Hendrix explained, "We've been trying to come up with a plan to take over the Kingdom. With Pike's help we might be able to pull it off. This is something we need to talk about together. We'll be outnumbered if we're caught." She glanced at Kibosh, knowing she'd tell them the real news she was avoiding saying: "That's not the only thing we were discussing."

Stamina was curious. "Is this about Pike's hired goons?"

Kibosh nodded. "That's right. Apparently, we know one of the people Pike might've hired."

Hendrix came clean: "Trinity might be one of the mercenaries."

Cross's demeanor changed for the worse. "Now I know why Kibosh was pissed off."

Stamina asked, "Why didn't you tell us before?"

Hendrix was honest: "This was a headache we didn't need right now. We have a lot at stake here. She knows we stay in New York, but she obviously didn't want trouble. She might be here just for Pike. I'm giving you all an order not to make a move on Trinity unless she becomes a threat."

Stamina looked at it as a blessing. "This might be an opportunity for us. We can take her out and get the Kingdom."

Kibosh disagreed, "Not exactly. If Trinity catches wind, we're after the Kingdom, she'll get in the way."

Cross was as clear as she was honest: "I'll stay out of her way until she pushes the wrong button. Then I'll bury her like I should've done years ago."

Kibosh agreed, "You have my vote."

Hendrix assured her team, "Trinity will die. Now isn't the time. Don't worry, she's not getting away from us again. It's only a matter of time."

Kibosh replied frustrated, "Let's hope your new friendship with Pike doesn't get in the way of our plans. Now we're after two things, the Kingdom and Trinity."

"I understand your concern, but I'll be the first to take care of Pike or Trinity if they become problems. The same goes for Boswell. I'm still the leader, Kibosh."

Kibosh barked back, "Let's hope so."

Stamina wanted answers: "So what's the plan?"

Hendrix answered, "Kibosh, I want you to take Stamina into the next town. See what you can find out. If Trinity's really in New York, you'll hear about it. Report back to me when you come up with something."

A rare smile came over Kibosh's face. "Consider it done."

Cross rose to her feet as she grabbed her assault rifle. "And me?"

Hendrix answered, "You're staying with me. We need to come up with a plan. When we locate Trinity, we need to make sure she can't interfere with our work. Nothing's stopping us from taking the Kingdom." For Hendrix, that aircraft meant everything, and it belonged to her.

TO BE CONTINUED.